Hard to Hold On To

Hard to Hold On To

A HARD INK NOVELLA

LAURA KAYE

AVONIMPULSE
An Imprint of HarperCollinsPublishers

Excerpt from *Full Exposure* copyright © 2014 by Sara Jane Stone.
Excerpt from *Personal Target* copyright © 2014 by Kay Thomas.
Excerpt from *Sinful Rewards 1* copyright © 2014 by Cynthia Sax.

EPub Edition AUGUST 2014 ISBN: 9780062339393
Print Edition ISBN: 9780062339409

10 9 8 7 6 5

*Dedicated to all those who serve and
the people who love them.*

Chapter 1

As THE BLACK F150 truck shot through the night-darkened streets of one of Baltimore's grittiest neighborhoods, Edward Cantrell cradled the unconscious woman in his arms like she was the only thing tethering him to life. And right at this moment, she was.

Jenna Dean was bloodied and bruised after having been kidnapped by the worst sort of trash the day before, but she was still an incredibly beautiful woman. And saving her from the clutches of a known drug dealer and human trafficker was without question the most important thing he'd done in more than a year.

He should feel happy—or at least happier—but those feelings were foreign countries for Easy. Had been for a long time.

Easy, for his initials E. C. The nickname had been the brainchild years before of Shane McCallan, one of Easy's Army Special Forces teammates, who now sat at the other end of the big backseat wrapped so far around Jenna's older sister, Sara, that they might need the Jaws of Life to pull them apart. Not that Easy blamed them. When you walked through fire and somehow came out the other side in one piece, you gave thanks and held tight to the things that mattered.

Because too often, when shit got critical, the ones you loved didn't make it out the other side. And then you wished you'd given more thanks and held on harder before the fires ever started raging around you in the first place.

Easy would fucking know.

The pickup paused as a gate *whirr*ed out of the way, then the tires crunched over gravel and came to a rough stop. Easy lifted his gaze from Jenna's fire red hair and too-pale face to find that they were home—or, at least, where he was calling home right now. Out his window, the red brick industrial building housing Hard Ink Tattoo loomed in the darkness, punctuated here and there by the headlights of the motorcycles belonging to some of the Raven Riders who'd helped Easy and his teammates rescue Jenna and take down the gangbangers who'd grabbed her.

Talk about strange bedfellows.

Five former Green Berets and twenty-odd members of an outlaw motorcycle club. Then again, maybe not so strange. Easy and his buddies had been drummed out of the Army under suspicious, other-than-honorable circumstances. Disgraced, dishonored, disowned. Didn't matter that his team had been seriously set up for a big fall. In the eyes of the U.S. government and the world, the five of them weren't any better than the bikers they'd allied themselves with, so they'd have a fighting chance against the much bigger and better-armed Church Gang. And, when you cut right down to it, maybe his guys weren't any better. After all, they'd gone total vigilante in their effort to clear their names, identify and take down their enemies, and clean up the collateral damage that occurred along the way.

Like Jenna.

"Easy? *Easy*? Hey, E?"

The voice reached him as if he were underwater— distant and indistinct. Blinking out of his thoughts, Easy turned to find three sets of eyes staring at him. Shane was already out of the truck and offering a hand to Sara. From the looks on their faces, it was pretty clear they'd been trying to get his attention for a while. Derek DiMarzio, another of his former SF teammates, had turned in the driver's seat to look at him, too.

"Okay, man?" Marz asked, his expression unusually serious. Normally, the guy acted like he was on a perpetual sugar high.

Easy was so far from okay, he didn't think he could get there with a fleet of cars and a limitless gas card. He gave a nod, popped open the door, and carefully guided Jenna and himself out. God, her weight and her warmth felt so good in his arms.

Shane and Sara met him at the back of the pickup, and Sara smoothed her hand over Jenna's forehead.

"Sweetie, it's me. You're okay. We're both okay," Sara

said, her voice cracking. Easy had some major respect for Sara—for both the Dean girls, really, because the Church Gang had put them through some serious hell the past few years yet they were still standing.

Shane wrapped his arms around Sara from behind, devotion and concern clear in his expression. "She'll be all right," he said, pressing a kiss into Sara's light red hair. "Let's get her inside so Becca and I can check her out." Though Shane's primary occupation on their team had been intelligence specialist, he was secondarily trained as a medic.

Swiping at her eyes, Sara nodded. "Yeah."

As their little group turned to cross the parking lot, three people burst out the back door of Hard Ink, a German shepherd puppy hot on their heels. Becca Merritt was an ER nurse, their deceased commander's daughter, and the reason Easy and his teammates had been reunited a week ago. She'd come to Nick Rixey—formerly the team's second-in-command and co-owner of Hard Ink—for help to find her missing brother, who had also been taken, as it turned out, by the Church Gang. Charlie Merritt was now safe and hanging back at the door, watching them. Next to Becca was Nick's younger brother Jeremy, who'd never been military but had still stepped up and helped them every way he could this whole past week.

"Marz radioed in that you'd gotten her, but it's really freaking good to see it with my own eyes," Becca said, running up to their group.

"They did it. Just like you said they would," Sara said, as they exchanged a quick hug.

While it sucked that the women had the kidnapping of a sibling in common, at least they had each other to turn to. Everybody should have the kind of friend who understood your fears, accepted you even at your weakest, and held you up even when you couldn't do that shit on your own. He'd had that, once, back when he'd been a better man than he was now. Behind his temple, pain throbbed in time with his pulse.

"Thank God it's over," Jeremy said, raking a heavily tatted hand through his dark hair.

The words settled a leaden weight on Easy's shoulders. Not by a fucking long shot. Hell, this snafu might never be over. "For tonight," he said.

Becca tucked her long, blond hair behind her ears and turned her attention to Jenna. Her expression went serious, and Becca's eyes focused as she scanned her gaze over the young woman's face. "I'll do an exam."

Take care of Jenna. Yes. Easy gave a nod, and they moved as a group across the lot. As long as he concentrated on Jenna, Easy found he could block everything else out, or at least dial it down. The aches that tightened his joints. The yearning for what he'd once had and who he'd once been. The insidious little thoughts that told him it would all be better if he could just fall the fuck to sleep—and not wake up again. Ever.

When they reached the back door of Hard Ink, Easy traded glances with Charlie, who'd scooped under his arm the three-legged puppy Becca had brought home, and they'd collectively named Eileen. Charlie had shaggy blond hair, dark circles under his eyes, and a bandaged hand following the gang's severing of two of his fingers before the team had rescued him five days ago. Church and his thugs had targeted the Merritt siblings because their father, Colonel Frank Merritt—Easy's former SF commander—had been dirty and somehow in bed with the gang, a fact Charlie had apparently gotten too close to revealing using some better-than-average hacking skills.

So their colonel's betrayals hadn't just rained down on Easy and his teammates. Sonofabitch

Charlie looked both relieved and uncomfortable as he held open the thick industrial door and watched Easy sidestep inside. No doubt, seeing Jenna put Charlie right back into his own experience with the Churchmen. Easy knew how that was. When you'd lived through a worst-case scenario come true, your mind became a little house of horrors, finding something that triggered the memories you most wanted to forget in every little thing.

Sometimes it made you question what it actually meant to survive.

Before the door clicked shut, the rumble of engines idling at the gate next to the building followed them in.

"Oh, God, please let that be Nick. Take her up. I'll be right there," Becca said, bolting back out the door. Before their operation had gotten under way earlier in the evening, the team and its biker allies had divided into two units with separate missions against the Churchmen at two different locations. B-Team's returning home safe from intercepting a large weapons sale would be a load off everyone's mind.

The loud revs of motorcycles sounded a minute later.

"You guys do your thing," Marz said. "I'll see if Nick and Beckett need help handling the Ravens."

"Roger that," Shane said, passing the darkened first-floor door to the tattoo parlor and rounding the bottom of the cement-and-metal steps. As they started upstairs to the floors where they were all crashing, Shane shook his head. "If you'd told me a week ago I'd be caught up in the middle of paying off hired thugs with stolen guns, I'd have told you to stop watching so many Jerry Bruckheimer movies."

"That's the fucking truth," Easy said, his voice gruff. And then he winced at the curse and his gaze cut to Jenna's face. Still out. *Have a little respect, Edward,* came the deep baritone of his father's voice from the depths of Easy's memory. His father was a deeply religious man and had had no tolerance for . . . well, much of anything wasn't an unfair way to put it.

Shane was right, though—the Ravens' assistance hadn't been free, and they were either gonna have to pony up the two-grand-per-rider fee or part with the assets that had been acquired in their confrontation with the Church Gang tonight. The guns were a windfall in more ways than one. First, since Nick's team had stolen them, they'd hurt the gang's bottom line and hopefully their reputation, too. Second, the guns represented assets that allowed the Hard Ink team to save their cash for a rainy day. And goddamnit it all to hell but it'd been pouring on them nonstop.

When they hit the landing, Shane reached for the keypad next to the door to Nick and Jeremy's big loft apartment. The refurb on the place kicked ass, but that wasn't where Easy wanted to go.

"She can have my bed," Easy said. "Apartment's pretty full, and my room will give her privacy." Besides, he couldn't sleep worth a motherfuck, so the bed was about as useful to him as a screen door on a submarine.

Shane's gaze cut to Sara to get the okay on the idea, and she gave a shaky nod. Easy started up, and the couple followed.

"You guys need help?" Jeremy asked from down below.

"Bring up my kit?" Shane called. "And let Becca know where we went."

"And a bucket or something?" Sara said. "In case she wakes up and gets sick."

"Got it," Jer said.

The mere idea of Jenna's pain made Easy's stomach roll in sympathy. He might've only known her a couple of days and talked to her a handful of times, but she'd been the first person since forever to look at and talk to him like he was just any regular fucking guy. For a single night, he'd been her protection detail. She hadn't known about his past or his failures or the black hole inside him, and it was so goddamn *freeing* that Easy had felt like he could fill his lungs for the first time in a year. In the course of a few hours, she'd sassed him, disobeyed him, and rolled her gorgeous blue eyes at him, and he'd . . . *felt*. Annoyance. Humor. Exasperation. Any and every frickin' one of those was light-years better than his norm. Her smiles and her feistiness and her sweet curves had made him feel like a whole man again. And it had all been such a fucking revelation that Easy hadn't been able to stop thinking about Jenna—or worrying about her—since.

How Easy wished he'd been able to *stay on* as protection for Jenna, so none of this would have happened to her, but they hadn't realized the danger was so great . . .

Guilt tossed Easy's gut.

Letting people down seemed to be his specialty.

At the next landing, Easy turned left and pushed through a door without a knob or any locking mechanism. Jeremy had been renovating the old warehouse a bit at a time, and the two big apartment spaces on the third floor were still works in progress. Beige cement floors and unpainted drywall stretched for miles, but the electricity and plumbing were good to go, and all this empty space had allowed Nick, Jeremy, the other SF teammates, and Becca and her brother Charlie places to crash for however long the team's investigation into the clusterfuckery of their past went on. And now Sara and Jenna were calling Hard Ink home, too.

The light over the unfinished kitchen counter guiding the way, Easy crossed the big rectangle that would one day become a living room and carried Jenna down the hall to the first room on the right. "Hit the light, would ya?"

Shane flicked the switch, casting a golden glow over the beige.

The windowless room's innards consisted of nothing more than a queen-size mattress-and-box-spring set perched on a metal frame. A duffel of Easy's clothes sat on the floor against one wall, along with a gray gun case.

His cell phone' charging cord hung from an outlet. The only color in the room came from the dark blue sheets and comforter tucked military tight around the mattress's four corners.

Settling Jenna on the bed, Easy regretted having to let go. Story of his life right there. He stepped back, clearing the way for Shane to crouch beside her.

Moments later, the twelve-by-twelve felt jam-packed. Jeremy had arrived with Shane's big first-aid kit, Charlie in tow, hanging back in the doorway again like he wasn't sure if he was welcome. Becca came soon after.

Easy didn't want to leave, but he didn't want to be in the way, either. He retreated to the hallway and leaned back against the wall like it was the only thing keeping him vertical. Jeremy and Charlie joined him a minute later. They shut the door behind them and settled side by side against the facing wall, Charlie in the same sweats and T-shirt he'd worn earlier in the day and Jeremy in another of his apparently endless supply of raunchy shirts. This one said, "Blink if you're horny."

"Long fucking night," Jeremy said, scrubbing his hands over his face. Letters on the backs of each of his fingers spelled out N-O-R-E-G-R-E-T. What Easy wouldn't give to feel that way. Just for five fucking minutes.

Cutting his gaze to Jer's light green eyes, Easy gave a nod. Not because he had the energy to do so but because it was damn rude not to respond when someone spoke directly to you.

"You're gonna be able to run a computer-security business on the side once all this is done. A regular Jer-of-all-trades," Charlie said, looking sideways at the guy like he was maybe a little shy. Then again, he was another recent kidnapping victim, two days out of surgery to clean up the butcher job the gang had done on his fingers, and one of the newest arrivals to their merry band of thieves—more than enough reasons to be a little reserved.

"No way, dude. Shit makes me so nervous, I wanna puke." Jeremy grinned at Charlie. "If we have to work together on it again, though, I'll try not to ralph on you."

Charlie chuckled under his breath. "Big of you."

"I aim to please," Jer said, elbowing the other guy.

When Charlie's cheeks went pink, and he ducked his head as if trying to hide the reaction behind the lengths of his blond hair, Easy tilted his own head back against the wall and closed his eyes. As the other two men continued to quietly talk, Jeremy occasionally throwing in some more flirting, Easy worked to tune them out. Not because he cared that some kind of attraction might be brewing between the two but because pretty much any and every show of friendship reminded him of everything he'd lost and therefore hurt like a motherfuck.

Easy wasn't sure how much time had passed when the door to his room opened, and Shane, Sara, and Becca came out. Glancing over Shane's shoulder, Easy caught a quick glimpse of Jenna lying on her back under the covers before the door cut off his view.

Shane put an arm around Sara's shoulders and met Easy's gaze. "She'll be okay. Woke up enough to recognize Sara, then was back out again. Probably feel like shit for the next twenty-four, but there's no evidence of broken bones or internal injuries from what we can tell. We cleaned up the lip and butterflied the cut by her eye." Shane's gray eyes flashed with the same anger eating through Easy's gut. She'd been struck in the face more than once if the busted lip and black eye were any indication. "Now we wait," Shane said with a sigh.

"Yeah," Sara whispered. And then she burst into tears.

"Aw, sweetness," Shane said as he folded her into his arms.

Sara cried like her soul had been ripped open. Shock, relief, four years of living hell being grieved, no doubt. The sound was filled with such mourning and agony that it made Easy a little dizzy—because it was a damn good aural representation of the way he felt inside. But Easy had never had the balls to give voice to it. Not once.

His instinct was to get away from all that raw emotion—and he could see on their faces that the other guys felt the same—but Shane and Sara were blocking their escape out of the narrow hallway. So there was a whole lot of looking down going on.

"I'm sorry. I'm okay," she said a few minutes later.

"I know, but you don't have to be," Shane whispered.

The urgent need to be alone suddenly hit Easy over the head.

"Why don't you all go downstairs and relax," Becca said, rubbing Sara's back. "I'll hang here in case Jenna needs someone."

"No," Easy said more gruffly than he intended. He just really needed them all to go. Now. "I'll stay. You've been sitting up with Charlie every night. I'll hang."

"I should stay in case she wakes up," Sara said in a weak, exhausted voice.

Cupping her face in his hand, Shane leaned down to look in her eyes. "You haven't slept much in days. Jenna's home and safe. Easy can text us if she needs us. Right, E?"

"Absolutely," he said, trying to breathe through his growing anxiety. Were the walls closing in?

The debate was clear on her expression. "I don't know . . ."

"How 'bout this? Sleep while she's sleeping. We'll only be one floor down and can come up anytime you want," Shane said. Easy's jaw clenched while they waited for her answer. He had no right at all to want to be alone with Jenna, but that didn't stop him from wanting it all the same.

Rubbing her eyes, Sara let out a long sigh. "I guess . . . okay."

Shane nodded and threw Easy an appreciative glance. "Thanks. Text if you or Jenna needs anything."

"Yeah. Of course." *Go. Now. There's not enough air for all of us.* Easy's heartbeat tripped into a sprint.

"Jeremy, do you have a little lamp we can bring up here?" Shane asked him. "She's gonna be disoriented when she wakes up, and a little less wattage than the overhead might be nice to leave on for her."

"Done," Jeremy said, pushing off the wall. He and Charlie took off like they were only too glad to leave. It got incrementally easier to breathe.

"I won't leave her," Easy said, meeting Sara's searching gaze.

"Thanks," she said with a quick nod.

And then, fucking finally, they were all walking away from him until they disappeared out the far door to the loft. The aloneness and stillness was like the barometric pressure rising after a storm, making it even easier to breathe and stand upright and push back the panic.

Except, how the hell was he going to be of any use to Jenna if the sound and sight of her sister crying fucked him up like that?

Noise at the front of the apartment drew his gaze again. Jeremy carried a small black lamp with a plain white shade. When he got close enough, he reached for the bedroom doorknob.

Easy held out a hand. "I'll take care of it. Uh, thanks," he added, to cushion the edge on his tone.

"Yeah, sure." Jer turned away, then stopped and looked over his shoulder. "I don't know exactly what happened out there, but I wanted to say you guys did good tonight."

Maybe. But Easy could never do good enough to make up for the past.

For not having his best friend's back when it mattered.

For not getting to Marcus in time.

For being helpless to do a damn thing as the life bled out of his teammate's gut and eyes.

Meeting the younger Rixey's gaze, Easy forced himself to nod. "Overdue for a win," he managed around the knot in his throat, gripping the lamp's pole so hard he feared he might break the damn thing.

"Yeah," Jeremy said, then left.

Easy gasped for air and tried to see the beige wall in front of him instead of the goulash that had been what remained of his friend's intestines. Abdominal wounds were fucking messy like that.

"I'm done, E. Tell her I love . . ."

Those last words were a brand on Easy's soul. He turned his body toward the wall and banged his head against the surface. Once. Twice. Three times.

When his lungs managed an in-out again, Easy figured that was as good as it was gonna get. Not waiting for the memories to replay once more, he pushed into Jenna's room—louder than he should've, but she didn't budge—and plugged the lamp into the outlet next to the bed.

He turned away again, but his gaze got snagged on Jenna's face, which lured him in. Stepping closer, Easy bent down, needing to see her chest rise and fall with his own eyes. Proof of life.

Wake up. Wake up and give me a hard time. Anything. Just give me your eyes.

She didn't, of course.

But Easy didn't miss the fact that the tightness in his chest eased off when he was close to her like this. Not that he was gonna be a creeper and sit in here and watch her sleep.

Stalking toward the door, he flicked off the overhead. From its position on the floor, the little lamp threw a much gentler glow over that corner of the room.

Pulling the door most of the way shut, Easy slid down against the doorjamb, putting his ear at the opening in case she cried out and his body between Jenna and the rest of the world.

Just in fucking case.

Chapter 2

EASY RIPPED OUT of the nightmare like the images in his subconscious were about to wrap their bony fingers around his throat. He was as disoriented as he was surprised he'd fallen asleep in the first place. Ass numb, back screaming, neck kinked, he shook his head in an effort to beat it all back.

A distressed whimper. Then another.

The sound worked where the physical motion hadn't. Easy was immediately and clearly awake.

Jenna.

He was off the cement and beside her in an instant.

Blue eyes flashed up to him with such fear and pain that it reached inside his chest and squeezed his heart.

Easy crouched by the bedside and held up his hands. "Jenna, it's Easy. Remember? You're all right. My guys— the ones you met the other night—we got you back. You're at a safe place. Sara's here, and she's okay, too," he rushed out in a soft voice.

Her eyes narrowed and darted from focusing on his face to a quick survey of her surroundings and back again. "E-E-Eas," she rasped, her voice a dry scrape.

Relief shot through his veins. "Yeah."

"Eas-y," she whispered. And then she threw her upper body off the edge of the bed and caught him around the neck. "Th-thank you," she said in a strangled tone.

Moisture where her cheek pressed against his. Trembling shoulders. Thick swallows. Jenna's crying both gutted Easy and built him up—because she didn't fear him. Instead, she'd turned to him for comfort. Yet she cried so quietly that he might not have heard it had her mouth not been so close to his ear.

"Don't you worry about a thing," he managed as he wrapped his arms around her shoulders. Slowly, he rose until his hip rested on the edge of the mattress.

Jenna pulled herself closer until she was sitting in a ball in his lap, her arms so tight around his neck and shoulders it was like she was holding on to him for dear life.

"Shh" he whispered as he stroked sweaty red hair off the side of her face. "You're okay now."

"Okay," she whispered against his throat. "Okay. Okay."

"Maybe I should go get Sara—"

"No!" A quick shake of her head against his. "Don't leave me."

No. He wouldn't. He'd left a friend once and knew all the ways that could go wrong. "I won't," he whispered.

Easy wasn't sure how long he sat there holding her, he only knew that at some point the tremors in her body stopped, her hold loosened, and her breathing evened out. She'd fallen asleep. In his arms.

That she'd found solace in him—a man who had no solace for himself—was the sweetest fucking thing he could ever remember experiencing. And it made him feel strong in a way he hadn't in what seemed like forever.

Knowing she needed rest above everything else, Easy slowly lowered them until Jenna lay on the edge of the bed. Half holding his breath, he gently slid his arms out from under her, his gaze on her face to see if his movements were disturbing her. But she stayed out cold.

And then he retreated to his place in the doorway. Only this time, he didn't fall asleep. His body and ears were tuned in to every little noise Jenna made and kept him wide-awake. In case she needed him again.

Needed.

How long had it been since he'd really been needed?

Actually, Easy didn't have to ask that question. The day the Army had handed down the other-than-honorable discharge that had kept him and his teammates out of Leavenworth but tossed them out of the military had been the last time before this week he'd really felt needed, valuable, like he mattered in the least. And Easy had his commander, Colonel Frank Merritt, to thank for every single way that his life had gone down the drain over the past twelve months. Not that he should complain since he still *had* a life. Six of his teammates—including Easy's own best friend, Marcus Rimes—hadn't been so lucky that day out on a dirt road in the middle of bum-fuck Afghanistan when a checkpoint had gone bad.

Though, if Easy was being honest, he often wondered who'd been the luckier parties that day. Those who'd lived or those who'd died?

Either way, the shit pie all of them were now forced to eat had been Merritt's doing since he'd betrayed the team, his own damn honor, and everything they'd all stood for by running a black op on the side for a coupla million in dead presidents.

Which was why, when Nick Rixey had called over a week ago, Easy almost hadn't come. What the fuck did he care if Merritt's kids were up to their necks in danger?

But the call—and especially Nick's feeling that what was going on with the Merritts somehow tied back to what had happened to the team and therefore might give them a lead—had lured Easy in with the possibility of being needed again. Useful again. Present in the world again.

None of which he had back home in Philadelphia, working for his father's auto parts store. He liked cars as much as the next guy, but stocking, tracking down, and distributing new- and used-car parts wasn't exactly a calling. It was a brainless, soulless activity that kept him functioning enough that no one looked too close or probed too deep. It was just a day-to-day, nine-to-fiver that gave him the bare minimum of a reason to open his eyes and get out of bed. And it contributed to the family business enough to keep his father from reminding him every five fucking seconds that Easy had ruined the good thing he'd had going.

Nick's call had rescued Easy from all that empty going through the motions that was his nonliving life. And maybe from acting on the dead-end thoughts that were becoming more and more intrusive and alluring.

Easy scrubbed his hands over his face and peered over his shoulder at Jenna. His eyes couldn't get enough of the contrast of her fiery hair against the pale cream of her skin. He sighed.

The damn irony was that Easy hadn't wanted to go into the Army. That had been his father's solution to the trouble Easy had gotten into as a teenager. At first, he'd been resentful as hell. Initially, he'd hated the orders and the barking drill sergeants and pretty much everything else about boot camp. But by the end of that training, Easy had found the promise of brotherhood and acceptance in a way he never had before. And *God* how he'd wanted it. He'd excelled at every other school and training required to go SF, and eighteen months later, came out wearing the beret.

The best of the best.

All gone now.

Jenna's moan drew his gaze across the room again. She'd pushed her upper body off the sheets and all that pale cream had disappeared in favor of a sickly green.

Easy scrabbled off the floor, grabbed the bucket, and lifted it just as Jenna threw up.

There wasn't much to catch.

But that didn't keep her body from dry-heaving over and over until Easy's gut clenched in sympathy. Jenna clutched the edge of the bucket and curled around it the same way she had his body earlier. He scooped her hair into a ponytail and held it back from her face. The red was just as striking against the dark brown of his skin. He wouldn't mind seeing it sprawled across his chest . . .

Easy cut that line of thinking off before it went somewhere absofuckinglutely inappropriate. Especially given how sick Jenna was. And, well, to be completely fair, how sick in the head he was. And those two were just for starters.

But, of course, his brain couldn't stop there with all the reasons that the two of them turning into something more than protector-protectee wasn't ever happening. Putting aside the fact that they barely knew each other, which wasn't nothing, their age difference was another reason. Easy had to have seven or eight years on the younger Dean sister. And, no doubt, the older sister wouldn't want some old, borderline criminal, definitely washed-out soldier for the sibling she'd fought so hard to protect. And honestly, having let Rimes die, how the fuck did Easy think he could do right by someone like Jenna? Which raised the fubar they found themselves in the middle of—couldn't forget that as a reason why that solace Easy found in Jenna's presence wouldn't be leading anywhere anytime soon. Not to mention that he lived three hours away—some days he couldn't get his ass out of bed let alone to try to have a long-distance relationship . . .

Spiral. Spiral. Spiral.

Easy excelled at the downward spiral of negative thoughts these days. Didn't matter if the thing he was sitting and spinning on wasn't even in the realm of the possible. Not really the point. The point was that everywhere he looked, he saw walls too damn high to climb even if he'd had the energy and the will to climb them, which he mostly didn't.

What a fucking prize he was.

"Thank you," she said on a raspy exhale. "Sorry."

"Not necessary," he said, forcing himself out of the tangle of his head and focusing on what mattered. "I'd offer you water, but I don't think you could keep it down."

The groan she unleashed was as much of an answer as he was gonna get. Jenna released the bucket and crumpled onto the bed.

When he was sure she was out again, he made a trip to the latrine down the hall, cleaned the bucket, and wet a cloth for her. Then he splashed his face with ice-cold water just to try to jar a little of the bullshit out of his head. He tugged his cell from his pocket and woke it up to see that it was after two in the morning.

"Easy!"

The shriek had his feet moving before his brain even processed Jenna's distress.

Eyes wide and face pale, her upper body was propped up by her elbows. Her gaze clawed onto him the minute he skidded into the room.

"I'm here. Right here." He dropped the bucket to the floor and resumed his position on the edge of the bed.

"I . . . I didn't know . . . I was . . ." She shook her head and swallowed thickly. "Don't leave me," she finally managed. "Please."

Needed. She needed him. Her fear and panic gutted

him, but if his presence could soothe that fear—if his presence could be a boon to another—that would . . . that would mean everything. "I'm not going anywhere. You need me, I'm here."

Jenna gave a quick nod and curled her whole body around Easy's where he sat on the bed, her thighs tucking against his lower back, her belly against his hip, her chest and face against his thigh. She grasped his hand and pulled it against her heart like a child cuddling a teddy bear.

And something about her trembling body and uncontrolled shudders and racing heart beat stilled all the shit in his mind.

Be there for her.

Purpose. Mission. Reason to be.

"Not going anywhere," he whispered around the knot suddenly lodged in his throat.

For a man who'd been standing so far out on a ledge he'd been dangling one foot over the great white nothingness, these things represented a lifeline. The whole damn week of being reunited with his team had promised the existence of such a thing, but right here, in this moment with Jenna Dean, Easy actually *found* it.

JENNA DEAN HAD thrown up so much she wasn't sure if she had any internal organs left, but since she still drew breath, she figured at least her lungs remained intact.

As many seizures as she'd had in her life, she'd *never*

gotten that sick for this long, which meant it hadn't all been from yesterday's seizure. It had been from what Bruno had given her.

Forcing her eyelids open was the only way to keep the memories of her capture and imprisonment from playing against the insides of her eyes, especially when her gaze immediately settled on the head and shoulders of the man who'd saved and taken care of her.

Easy.

Through a warped, blurry memory, she could see him lifting her into his arms and pulling her in against his broad chest. When had that happened? Or maybe she'd dreamed it?

No, she didn't think so.

How long had she been in this room? And where *was* this room anyway? She had no sense of time or place whatsoever.

She only knew that, wherever she was and however long she'd been here, Easy had been right by her side the whole time. Now, he sat on the floor, his back against her bedside, his head hanging loose on his thick, broad shoulders as if he were asleep.

The man barely knew her, and yet second to Sara, he'd been there for her more than any other person on the planet. He'd seen her at her absolute worst, likely an understatement given how much she'd puked and how she *had* to smell, and yet, here he still sat.

Any man willing to handle the tears and vomit of a strange woman to whom he owed absolutely nothing was someone worth getting to know better. That *had* to be in a girls' guide to guys somewhere.

The thought might've made Jenna smile if her lips weren't so dry and there wasn't a stinging pull on the one side of her mouth. From backhand number two, as she recalled. Which she really *didn't* want to do if she could help it.

Curled in a ball facing him, Jenna pushed her hand across the blue bedding and laid her fingers on his shoulder. Wiggled them a little.

Nothing.

Poor guy. If she'd been up all night catching someone's puke in a bucket, she'd be passed out right about now, too.

Thinking about how Easy had cared for her made Jenna think about her older sister. Sara's whole life the past four years had been about taking care of and keeping Jenna safe—no matter the cost. And, oh, God, the cost had been high. So high. Just thinking about everything Sara went through after their father's death—imprisonment, rape, the forced labor to the Church Gang, the constant threat that had hung over their heads, unbeknownst to Jenna—all of it hurt Jenna's heart so bad she was sure someone had reached inside her chest and squeezed the organ with all their might.

Ever since Jenna had learned all the horrors Sara had endured—for *her*—she'd had random moments where it was suddenly hard to breathe. Sara had been caught in the middle of a living hell, and Jenna had been going to freaking college and worrying about things like tests and grades and annoying professors and what'd happened at Saturday night's party. Like any of that actually mattered.

How would Sara ever forgive her for not knowing, not realizing, not helping?

Jenna couldn't begin to answer that question because she would *never* forgive herself.

What kind of person didn't know her sister had been raped? What kind of person didn't know her sister's back bore a mass of scars from a brutal whipping? What kind of person didn't know her sister was being *forced* to do her skeevy job waitressing at a strip club and be with her Neanderthal of a "boyfriend"?

What kind of person actually *blamed* her sister even the littlest bit for any of those situations?

Nausea rolled through Jenna's belly. She smothered her groan in the sweat-dampened pillow beneath her. The movement of her face against the soft cotton set off a throbbing ache around her whole eye. From backhand number one.

When the worst of the sensation passed, she inched closer to Easy. He had muscles so well-defined, their contours revealed themselves through the Under Armour shirt he wore. Even sitting there relaxed, his shoulders were like a mountain. He was tall, too. Well, pretty much any guy was compared to her, but Easy was the kind of big that gave you the feeling he could shield you from the brunt of a bad storm. And his skin was the richest, darkest, most perfect shade of brown.

Slowly, softly, she dragged her fingers to the bare skin

on the back of his neck. She let her hand rest there, skin to skin, cupping his warmth and strength against her palm. There was something truly beautiful and compelling about the contrast of her skin against his.

Jenna knew it the instant he woke up because the muscles under her fingers flinched and tensed. Heat roared into her cheeks. How being caught admiring him could embarrass her after she'd vomited in the man's presence all night, she wasn't sure, but it did. She withdrew her hand.

"Don't," he said, voice tense and gruff.

"Sorry," she whispered, pulling farther away.

"No, I meant don't . . . stop. I don't mind," he said, one shoulder lifting in the barest shrug.

For some reason, the invitation in his words made the idea of touching him feel intimate in a way it hadn't moments before. She stroked her fingers up his neck to the close-shaved black hair of his head. The shortness of his hair was almost ticklish against her skin. "Have you ever worn it completely bald?" she asked, as her hand gently palmed the back of his head. She wasn't sure why she was engaging a freaking former soldier who had protected her and saved her life in a conversation about hairstyles, of all things, except maybe that she was curious about him.

Curious about every part of him.

"Nah," he said. "Too high-maintenance."

The words beckoned her smile. She sucked in a quick breath at the pulling sting on her lip.

Easy turned to face her, wearing a concerned frown. Dark circles marred the skin below tired, deep brown eyes. He looked exhausted and wary and not a little pissed off. Sexy. Intimidating. "What's the matter?" His voice reflected the concerned-tired-angry combo, but it didn't seem like the anger was directed at her.

"Uh." So many potential answers surged forward in response to his question, she couldn't say anything intelligent at all. Her gut and back hurt from all the heaving. Her throat was raw. Random spots on her arms hurt from how roughly she'd been handled. Finally, she licked dryly at the corner of her lip and winced. "Just stings."

His gaze tracked the movement, and despite how dreadful she felt, her body reacted to his interest. Her pulse jumped, her cheeks heated again, her belly flipped, especially when his gaze remained locked on her lips. Maybe it was the chemistry that had simmered between them the other night when he'd protected her at her apartment. Maybe it was her gratitude for being saved, or maybe it was how jumbled everything felt in her head after the total whirlwind of the past few days, but Jenna would've given anything for a fresh mouth and a clean body so she could kiss him. And maybe other things. Definitely other things.

If her kidnapping had taught her anything, it was to live in the moment. Because who the hell knew when a gangbanger was going to bust down your door, grab you in broad daylight, and stuff you in the back of a van. And then you'd never once get to experience all the things you'd waited to do, to try, to have.

Except Easy had rescued her and given her a second chance.

His brown eyes flashed to hers and went absolutely molten. "You're hurt, Jenna."

"Feeling better," she managed.

Those eyes narrowed. "And you've been through a lot."

"All over. Thanks to you," she whispered. "Easy, I just—"

Knock, knock, knock.

Easy flew to his feet as the door pushed open, and Sara peeked in.

"You're awake," Sara said, green eyes filled with both relief and concern. "Can I come in?"

Jenna nodded and threw some effort into scooting into a sitting position, her back against the unpainted wall. "What is this place?"

"It's . . . well, kind of a long story. Shane and Easy's team are using this building as a base to stage an investigation. There's a tattoo parlor on the first floor that one of the guys owns. Most of the rest of it is unfinished, like this." Sara shrugged and shook her head. "How are you?"

Jenna frowned. "Oh, uh, okay. Mostly."

From behind Sara, Easy crossed his arms, arched an eyebrow, and gave her a pointed look that said if she didn't spill, he would.

Hadn't she done enough spilling? Which she guessed explained the hard-assed look. She sighed, not really wanting to burden Sara any more than she'd already done. For *years* now. "I got sick a few times."

That eyebrow was still hitched in disapproval. What a hard-ass! Who'd saved her. And cleaned up her puke. So, okay.

"Well, actually, I got sick a lot of times. Like, I couldn't stop dry-heaving most of the night. But I feel much better now," she rushed to add. Her gaze cut to Easy's, and she threw him a *There. Satisfied?* look. He gave a single nod.

All of Sara's delicate features dipped into a frown. "How many seizures did you have? How bad? I packed your medicine, so that might help."

Her medicine. She wasn't sure she should take it—at least not yet. But if she refused, then she'd have to explain *why* she was refusing something she knew she needed. And that meant telling Sara everything that had happened on the second day she'd been held by Bruno, Sara's not-really boyfriend/gang leader/all-around lowlife. And that wasn't something Jenna really wanted to do, especially as another knock sounded against the door.

"It's Shane. I brought Jenna's prescription like you asked," he said from out in the hall.

"Mind if Shane comes in?" Sara asked.

Shane's presence made Jenna question for the first time how the hell she was dressed. Funny that she'd never once wondered or worried about that when it had been just her and Easy. Her gaze dropped down to her chest and she lifted the navy comforter to see what was going on down on the bottom half. Same T-shirt and yoga pants she'd had on the day Bruno had kidnapped her. God, when Jenna had the chance to change, she was having these clothes burned immediately. She'd *never* be able to wear them again despite the fact that she adored this vintage Lenny Kravitz concert T-shirt because, well, it was *Lenny*. What more needed to be said, really?

A hand fell on her knee, making Jenna jump.

"Jen?" Sara prompted.

Jenna blinked. "Uh, sure."

Shane stepped through, and his smile shifted from hesitant to full when he looked at her. "Welcome back, Jenna," he said with the hint of a Southern accent. Tall, with light brown hair that looked like he constantly ran his fingers through it, Shane was so handsome he was almost pretty.

Her gaze flickered to Easy, who radiated none of Shane's charm or warmth, just a stone-cold protectiveness that made it easier for Jenna to breathe—exactly what she needed right now. "Thanks," she said to Shane, though the word felt grossly inadequate. But she had to say something because no doubt Shane had been involved in whatever they'd had to do to get her back from Bruno.

Sara smiled up at Shane as she accepted the white pharmacy bag and a bottle of water. And with that one look, that one brief exchange, Jenna knew. Sara was in love with him. Jenna had *seen* Sara fake a relationship for four years, so she knew what her sister looked like in that situation. She wasn't seeing any of that here. Her sister's body relaxed in Shane's presence and gravitated toward his. Her smile was full and easy, not at all forced. And she didn't think she was reading Shane wrong in seeing a lot of the same signs from him.

Tears pricked the backs of Jenna's eyes. Somehow, in the midst of all the crap, Sara had found a bit of happiness. Nobody deserved it more.

"Hey, are you okay?" Sara asked, scooting closer.

"What? Yeah, sure."

"Sweetie, I was talking to you, and you didn't even hear me." Sara slipped her hand into Jenna's.

Pulling her hand away, Jenna grimaced. "You don't want to touch me, I promise you. Not without a HazMat suit."

"Stop it. I don't care about that," Sara said, taking her hand again. "But I do need to know what happened."

"Why? It's over, right? I'm fine. Really." A thought hit her over the head, and Jenna gasped. "What happened to Bruno? Do you think he'll find us here? We should get out of the city—"

"Bruno's gone," Sara said.

Gone. The word froze the frenzied thoughts darting around inside Jenna's head. "Gone. Gone how?"

A series of emotions flitted over Sara's face. "He's, uh . . ."

"Dead," Easy said from the post he'd taken up against the wall by the door. "You won't have to worry about him anymore. Neither of you."

A moment of shock, then a whole torrent of relief. "Thank you," she said, meeting Easy's roiling gaze, as if he were almost daring her to disapprove. Hell to the no chance of that. "Thank you," she said again. The words remained inadequate no matter how many times she said them.

He stuffed his hands into the pockets of his jeans and ducked his head. And a part of Jenna wished it could just be the two of them here again. Easy had a quiet way about him that was peaceful and comforting, even though—clearly—the man was seriously and unabashedly lethal.

"So, then, it really *is* over," Jenna said. "You're free, Sara."

"Yeah," she said with a little smile that soon fell. Her grip tightened around Jenna's hand. "Please tell me what happened," she whispered. "I . . . if you don't . . . my mind goes right . . . to the worst . . ." Her words drifted off, but Jenna knew what she was thinking. Because, unlike her, Sara had actually lived through the worst.

So, no matter how much she wanted to just put what happened behind her, Jenna wasn't getting out of this. She owed it to Sara to put her mind at ease.

Fine. Then she'd stick to the highlight reel. Or would that be the lowlights?

Jenna inhaled deeply and let out a long breath. "Okay. They busted into our apartment, grabbed me, backhanded me when I tried to fight back, which is how I got this," she said, pointing to her right eye. The way it throbbed, it had to be black-and-blue. As the words poured out, Jenna's heart tripped into a panicky sprint. Just recounting what had happened—even in this cursory way—put her mind and body right back in the moment. She rushed to get it all out. "And then they tied me up in the van and held a gun on me. When we got to Confessions, they took me downstairs, and when I saw the black room, I had a seizure, and I don't remember much of anything until I woke up in darkness so total I couldn't see anything."

Sara's breathing hitched, and her eyes pooled with unshed tears.

And that reaction confirmed Jenna's suspicion that it was the same room Sara had been held in four years before. Sara hadn't given her too many details about what had happened to her during the week of her captivity, but she had mentioned a black room that deadened your senses and left you disoriented. After a seizure, especially a big one, Jenna needed no help whatsoever with disorientation, thank you very much. Damn epilepsy had that little nugget of awesomeness covered.

"Anyway, then a while later an older man brought me food. I didn't eat it because I didn't trust it. And then a while after that these two goons came and got me and I almost escaped, which is how I got this," she said, pointing to the corner of her mouth. Her right cheek was none too happy either, but it didn't feel swollen to the touch. And, really, who knew where the hit to the eye left off and became the hit to the mouth. She released a shaky breath and mentally jumped over a whole lotta stuff, hoping against hope that Sara would be satisfied with what she had shared. "And then I vaguely remember seeing Easy's face before I woke up here. So, yeah, that's about it."

There. Done.

Jenna's stomach did a loop-the-loop as her gaze cut from Sara's concern and confusion to Shane's scowl to Easy's rigid fury. The guy looked wound so tight that a flick of her finger might snap him in two.

"God, Jenna, I'm so sorry," Sara said, her voice cracking. "This is all my fault."

"No, it's not, Sara. It's never been your fault." Jenna would regret 'til her dying breath whatever role she'd played in ever making her sister believe otherwise.

Shane stepped up behind Sara and laid a hand on her

shoulder. "I agree. The real miracle is that Bruno didn't go off the deep end sooner."

"Okay," Sara said after a minute. "Okay." She blew out a breath. "I guess, though, what I don't understand is why you're still so sick if your only seizure happened more than twenty-four hours before we got you back."

"I don't know. Just a bad one, I guess," Jenna said, dropping her gaze to her lap and picking at the edge of the sheet. God, she hated lying.

"Well, as long as you're feeling better, that's all that matters," Sara said. "Here." She handed her the bottle of water. "I'd take it slow, though."

Jenna gave a small chuckle. "Yeah. No kidding." She uncapped the water and tilted the bottle to her lips. And, oh God, the cool moisture was luxurious against the aridity of her mouth and throat. She snuck another sip— and her gaze snagged on Easy. Who was looking at her with narrow eyes and a tilted head. Like he was analyzing her. Or doubting her. She blinked away. Probably just her own guilty conscience talking.

"Here, take this." Sara offered a pill in the cradle of her palm.

And Jenna's stomach began a slow, sinking descent. Her medicine. Which she really shouldn't take until she allowed plenty of time for whatever they'd given her to get out of her system. So many regular drugs—hell, even some foods—caused bad interactions with her antiepileptic meds, so she had no doubt that what they'd given her not only had an equal or better chance of doing the same but was also probably why she'd felt so sluggish and been so sick. Her brain went haywire enough without adding recreational drugs into the mix.

Which was why she avoided such things like the plague.

Then again, Bruno and his goons really hadn't asked for her opinion. More than that, one of them had slapped a big, beefy palm over her mouth and nose to force her to stop expressing it and swallow what they'd given her.

For some reason, it was the memory of that man's hand across her mouth and against her nose—smothering her until she thought her lungs would explode—that removed every last inch of the distance she'd shoved between her rote description of what had happened and the completely irrational but no less avoidable feeling that it was about to happen again *right this very minute*.

Ice-cold terror slammed into her out of nowhere. Her heart raced, her breathing shallowed, white spots played around the edge of her vision, and her fingertips went tingly.

"Jenna?" Sara said. The alarm in her sister's voice only made her panic worse. "Sweetie?"

Voices that Jenna couldn't interpret. Motion she couldn't make sense of. She grasped at her chest, sure her heart wouldn't be able to beat this hard much longer.

Her throat narrowed. Her chest tightened. Her breathing screamed as it sawed in and out of her windpipe.

Warmth. On her hand. On her face. She turned into it. And found Easy looking into her eyes. Intense. Focused. Determined.

"E . . . E . . . E . . ."

"Don't talk. Just breathe. But slow it down. Can you do that for me?" As she watched, he inhaled an exaggerated breath and slowly blew it out. Then again. And again. Needing him to ground her, she grabbed his arm as she gulped for breath and tried to pace her inhalations with his, using his steady, deep in and out as a metronome of peace and life. After a few minutes, it worked. Staring into his eyes, Easy talked her through the panic, helped her slow her breathing, and gently pulled her back from the brink. "There you go. You're just fine. No worries here. I gotchu."

He has me. Inhale. *He has me.* Exhale. *He has me.*

Jenna nodded. Suddenly, the need to purge every bit of her experience from her soul flooded through her. It almost felt like if she didn't get it all out, it might stain her forever. On the next exhale, she unleashed the words she knew she wouldn't be able to say unless she did it right now. And given what she yet had to admit, it was somehow easier saying it to someone other than Sara.

"I can't take my meds. They held me down and forced me to swallow something. A drug." Hot tears spilled down her cheeks. "I don't . . . know . . . what it was. I tried to fight. I did. But then it hit me, and it was like a lead blanket, or maybe a magic carpet, because I was flying but so damn relaxed I couldn't move my limbs. And then the one guy . . . he, um—" She shuddered and gooseflesh sprung up over her skin. God, she wished she could hold this part in. Hadn't Sara suffered enough? But the words were right there and falling from her tongue. "—t-touched me, just to prove he could and there wasn't a thing I could do to stop him." Just saying the words brought back the remembered feel of big, rough hands groping and squeezing her breasts.

A gasp sounded out from next to her.

Easy's only reaction was a ticking muscle in his jaw, as if he were clenching his teeth. "Did he—"

"No," she blurted. Jenna couldn't bear to hear him ask the question she knew he'd ask. Not in front of Sara. Not given what Sara had gone through. "Bruno made him stop." She gasped for air. "I didn't want . . . I didn't . . ." She shook her head—or maybe that was just her whole body shaking. Tears streamed down her face. "I didn't," she said again, Easy's intense gaze, warm, solid touch, and understanding words like a lifeline.

"'Course you didn't," he said. "All over now."

"Over." She nodded. "Thank you." Jenna tried to hug herself, but her arms only half obeyed. "I can't stop shaking. Could you . . . would you . . ."

Strong arms pulled her against a warm, broad chest. And as all those masculine muscles wrapped themselves around her, Jenna could finally draw a full, deep breath for the first time in maybe ten minutes.

Which allowed her to remember that Sara and Shane were here, too. And had no doubt just heard what Jenna had revealed. She turned her head to the other side, otherwise remaining tight against Easy's heat, and found

Sara hovering just behind her, an absolutely stricken expression on her pretty face.

Guilt flooded Jenna's gut for piling on to the load Sara already carried—*had been carrying* for years. No matter what Jenna did, it seemed she just couldn't stop hurting the one person she loved most in the world. She couldn't stop being a burden.

Chapter 3

TOUCHING JENNA WAS the only thing holding Easy together. Or, at least, keeping him from tearing the Sheetrock off the wall studs with his bare hands.

They'd fucking hit her, imprisoned her, drugged her, and touched her.

Some of that Easy had known. Some he hadn't. But hearing the words spill from her lips and watching her struggle to hold her emotions in check had made Easy go a little insane.

It almost made him wish Bruno weren't dead. Because Easy would've loved to be the one who'd actually taken the scumbag out. Of the three members of the team who'd been lying in wait for Bruno to appear, Shane had had the clearest shot. The mission was what had been most important, not whose bullet had exploded the cocksucker's brains all over his SUV's passenger seat. But, right now, in the heat of this moment, Easy wouldn't have minded having the chance to paint his hands in Bruno's blood as he watched the life drain from the lowlife's eyes.

Heaving a deep breath, Easy lifted his gaze—and found Sara and Shane staring at him. Or, more precisely, staring at how he was holding Jenna. He suddenly felt uncertain, like maybe he'd inserted himself somewhere he shouldn't have, like maybe he didn't belong. All he'd known was that Jenna was in deep distress and needed an anchor before it pulled her under.

And he'd wanted to be that for her.

He'd *needed* to be that for her.

But maybe calming her and helping her and holding her wasn't his place.

Well, duh. None of that was his place. But maybe Shane and Sara thought so, too.

His muscles screamed in protest, but Easy forced himself to loosen his hold and gently push himself away.

Jenna's fingers dug into his back, her hold tightening in direct proportion to how much he let go.

I gotchu. That's what he'd said.

So was he really going to walk away now?

His gaze cut back to Sara.

The small, sad smile she gave him was all the permission he needed. "Thank you," she whispered.

Easy pulled Jenna's weight firmly back against him. Her side against his chest. Her head against the crook of his neck. Her knees resting against his thigh. He wasn't sure how many minutes passed before Jenna's scratchy voice broke the silence.

"I'd like to take a shower," she said.

"Of course," Sara said with a smile that was just a watt too cheerful. "Probably make you feel a lot better."

It was one of those things that people said that was as untrue as it was polite.

"Yeah," Jenna said, easing away from Easy's chest. And though she gave his hand a squeeze as if to silently express gratitude, she didn't give him her eyes. Instead, she scooted away and slowly slid her feet off the edge of the bed to the floor. His loss of her heat and touch was nearly as wrenching as an amputation, a horrible analogy given that one of their teammates had actually suffered exactly that.

"Just go slow," Sara said, taking Jenna's arm. "Probably gonna be wobbly."

Jenna nodded, then slowly pushed herself into a standing position. Seeing her on her feet again filled Easy with reassurance and satisfaction. She really would be okay.

And then she won't need you anymore.

Spiral, spiral, spiral.

"You want to try to eat or drink something when you're done?" Sara asked, guiding her one step at a time away from where he sat on the bed, his back against the cold, hard wall.

"Maybe," Jenna said.

And then the sisters stepped through the door and out of the room. Easy stared at the empty doorway and tried to beat back the despair that threatened at the loss of everything he'd found in Jenna's presence. Stupid, really. He'd known the danger of his dependence when he'd first felt it, and he was feeling the evidence of that danger right now.

Because she wasn't his to need, to want, to depend upon.

Shane's gaze was suddenly a physical weight on Easy's face. The last thing Easy wanted was a too-perceptive intelligence officer putting his skills to work on him, so he got off the bed and rubbed the heels of his hands against his eyes.

"You were great with her, E. Thank you," Shane said.

Dropping his hands, Easy met his teammate's gaze and shrugged. "Just doing what anyone would do."

Chuffing out a humorless laugh, Shane shook his head and crossed his arms. "Well, that's some bullshit."

The black hole in the center of Easy's chest was making itself known again. To distract himself from the pain and Shane's inquisitiveness, he tore off his shirt, dropped it to the floor, and grabbed a new one from his duffel. "And what's that supposed to mean?" he asked as he tugged an old, soft gray hoodie over his head.

"Just what I said. Calling things how I see 'em, and what I've seen since the moment you took Jenna out of my arms last night was a man feeling all kinds of protective over a woman—"

"Again. Like *anyone* would be."

Shane threw up his hands. "Okay, E. Whatever you say. You want to play it like that, I won't push. But since you don't have any special interest here, how 'bout we let Beckett take the next shift with Jenna."

Heat roared through Easy's brain, and he spun on his heel.

The barely suppressed smirk and arched eyebrow told Easy he'd walked right into that one.

"Fuck you," Easy bit out, moving to push by the guy.

Shane grabbed his shoulder and blocked his exit. "Aw, don't be like that, man. I came clean to you about Sara."

"That was different," Easy said, muscling back the anger but feeling it clawing at him from the inside out. He didn't want to take Shane's head off. He really didn't. After all, it wasn't Shane's fault that Easy's emotional bank was so empty that he couldn't stand being teased about wanting something he could never have.

The guy's gray eyes narrowed and drilled into Easy's. "What's going on?"

A quick shake of his head. "*Nada.*"

His brows cranked down. "Easy, it's *me.*" Shane studied him for a long minute, then came out with, "Most of my life, I've felt responsible for the abduction of my eight-year-old sister."

The admission was like a sucker punch to the gut because Easy knew what Shane was trying to get him to do. Easy respected the hell out of Shane McCallan—for his ability to say what he'd said and a whole lot more—but there wasn't a snowflake's chance in hell that Easy was pulling up a chair to circle time and sharing his boo-boos.

He let that shit out, and he might never get it back in its box.

Not that it was too well secured as it was, but whatever.

"Wasn't your fault," Easy finally managed to say. "Now I gotta ask you to back off."

Shane gave a nod and a slap on his teammate's shoulder. "All right. I'm here, though. You know that, right?"

"Yeah. Now, why don't we give the women some privacy and clear out of here?" Last thing he wanted to do, really.

"Roger that." They made their way through the apartment and down the industrial stairs. "You up for a debrief?" Shane asked.

"Always," Easy said, glad for something operational to think about, something outside his head. Outside himself.

At the door across from the Rixeys' apartment, Shane entered a code into a keypad. The cavernous space on the other side of the door still looked like an old warehouse but had become their war room, their mess hall, and the space where everyone tended to congregate in general. Gym equipment filled the whole front half of the room, and Easy eyeballed a treadmill that had his name all over it. Nothing like a good, hard, long run to level him out and take the edge off.

In the front far corner sat a long, makeshift table made of plywood and sawhorses, and in the rear sat their operations center, which consisted of a row of computers and monitors and several big bulletin boards and whiteboards covered with maps and mug shots and lists and unanswered questions.

Per usual, Marz, the team's techy guru, sat at the center of it all, stacks of files and papers that made sense only to him all over the top of the makeshift desk. Standing around him drinking coffee and shooting the shit were Charlie, Nick, and Beckett Murda, the last of his surviving SF teammates.

Easy hadn't seen Nick and Beckett since before last

night's op. He approached Nick first, exchanging a hand clasp and a shoulder bump with the guy responsible for hauling his ass down from Philly. "Good work last night," Easy said. "Sounded like a big take."

The guy's pale green eyes were a striking contrast with his dark brown hair. "Right back atcha. Took some balls to take out Confessions the way you did, but it was the right damn call."

"Couldn't agree more," Beckett said, as they repeated the greeting. Linebacker big, always serious-faced, and scarred all around his right eye from a grenade explosion, Beckett was their gadget man. A mechanical device didn't exist that he couldn't build, rebuild, or improve upon.

Weapons and explosives? Now that was Easy's gig. When his team had gone to Confessions the night before to rescue Jenna from where they'd learned she was being held, E had brought along some C-4 in case the shit went south. As shit was wont to do. And south it had gone.

Jenna wasn't where their intel had said she should be. Instead, they found an informant who'd helped them dead from multiple stab wounds to the chest. And then they'd learned that Bruno had taken her with him to the gun deal.

Easy's rage had gone nuclear, and the deep need to take Confessions *out* so the Church Gang could never again use it to hurt Jenna, Sara, or any other woman had been all-consuming.

The thought made Easy antsy to know if what he'd done had worked. He ticked off his thoughts on his fingers. "Way I see it, we need a status update on the Church Gang. Whether the explosion leveled Confessions. What the impact of your raid on the gun deal is for them. What Church is doing and where he is." One by one he met each of the other men's eyes. "You know we gotta take him out before all this is said and done, right? He's gotta be plotting some hard-core revenge, which means he'll be looking for us. We need to find him first."

"I agree across the board," Nick said, surveying the group and finding them unanimous. There wasn't any official hierarchy or structure among them, yet they'd still fallen into their old pattern of looking to him since he'd once been their second-in-command. And why not? The guy was sharp, clearheaded, and had killer instincts. And Easy sure as hell didn't want the mantle of leadership.

Marz spun his chair toward them, a sheaf of papers in hand. "Way ahead of you. Miguel's already working on a damage assessment of Confessions," he said, referring to Nick's retired BPD friend who'd been assisting them with manpower and intelligence wherever he could. Miguel Olivero's assistance was even more important since they'd dug up more than one piece of evidence over the past week that the Church Gang had the authorities in their pocket, which took the police off the table as potential allies as long as Church remained an important player. "Ike and the Ravens are going to put out feelers to see what they can learn about Church and the gang's reputation, but they're also feeling the need to lie low while the dust settles, so they don't get hit with too much blowback."

"Don't blame 'em for that," Easy said. Even though Nick and Jeremy had known Ike Young for years, it had taken Easy a while to trust the tattooist/biker and come around to the idea that an outlaw motorcycle club could be useful to them. But when he next saw Ike, he was gonna owe the guy a serious apology. Without Ike's hooking them up with the Ravens, the team's wins from last night wouldn't have been possible.

Damn if the lines between the good guys and the bad guys weren't blurred by every part of this clusterfuck.

"Agreed," Nick said. "I think we should do the same. At least for the next day or two."

Easy was down with that. At the pace they'd been going the last week, a little R&R would ensure that people's heads were clear and their bodies ready to meet the next challenge that came their way.

Charlie cleared his throat. Easy wasn't sure if the guy was just shy or reserved or more comfortable with computers than with people, but he never said much. When he did? It was always worth listening to. "My landlord's son works with the city's gang commission. He might be able to help."

"The Jacksons," Beckett said, placing his empty coffee cup on a folding chair. "We met them while we were looking for you."

"Yeah," Marz said, holding up a thick booklet in one hand and kneading his right thigh with the other. Easy frowned. Marz had lost everything below that knee to the same grenade that had fucked up Beckett's eye, but the guy never complained and seemed to have adjusted well to the prosthetic, so it was almost easy to forget he wore it. Damn, if they all weren't experts at keeping their shit bottled up and battened down. "That's where we got this dossier on the Church Gang."

"It's a good idea, Charlie, but Easy's right," Nick said. "Church is very likely going to be putting his own feelers out, specifically looking for people asking around about his organization. Which means we'd need to be very careful about utilizing civilian resources any more than we have to."

Beckett nodded and crossed his thick arms. "I'll stock up on burn phones. We use a clean one every time we contact them. But Louis Jackson was a wealth of knowledge that night. I think Charlie's onto something there. And it's Jackson's *job* to be nosy about gangs, so that ought to provide him at least some cover."

The blond shifted his position against the desk and ducked his head, as if uncomfortable with everyone's talking about him.

"What else?" Nick asked.

"I have a whole list of research queries to work on," Marz said. "Charlie's gonna help me, then Jeremy will jump in around his clients. Keep you posted if and when we find our next big leads."

Murmurings of agreement and offers to help rose from all around the room.

"I have something I'd like to say," Shane said, stepping forward and tapping his fingers against the desk. "I know protecting Sara and rescuing Jenna were tangential to our main mission here—"

"Shane—"

"No, Nick. This needs to be said." Shane planted his hands on his hips, and Nick nodded for him to continue. "Every person in this room is sacrificing his safety, his income, and his job to be here. We're all doing it to get to the bottom of the whatthefuckery that killed our friends and tarnished our honor. It means a lot to me—" The sound of a thick swallow drew Easy's gaze to his friend's face. More than a little emotion was visible there. "What y'all did . . . and that you were willing to do it . . . for them and for me, it means a lot."

"We're family," Nick said simply, as if that said everything. And it did, didn't it?

"Family," Beckett said, nodding.

"You know it, McCallan. Dysfunctional misfits and all," Marz said, pushing out of his chair enough to clasp hands with Shane from across the desk. "Charlie, that includes you, too," he called over his shoulder.

"Oh, sure," Charlie said with a smirk. "Why does the computer nerd get lumped in with the misfits?" Despite the sarcasm, his expression was more than a little appreciative, and Easy could imagine why. It didn't sound like Charlie's father had been very accepting of the fact that Charlie was gay. From what Easy had heard, Merritt had been a real asshole about it, actually. Given the tension that existed between Easy and his own father, he knew what it meant to find and make your own family—one that accepted you for who you were.

"Hey, you're in good company," Beckett said, pointing at Marz, who flipped him in the bird in return.

Chuckles went around the room.

Even Easy managed to laugh. Because what Marz had said fit him to a T.

"Family," Easy said in a low voice, the emotion of the moment making him miss Rimes so bad, it was a physical pain in his chest. But even with that acute reminder of what he'd lost, Easy took a small measure of comfort. Because, this . . . *this* was the meaning and the belonging Easy had been missing for the past year.

"YOU OKAY IN there?" Sara asked from out in the hall.

The hot water of the shower rained down on Jenna's head. She'd finished bathing herself at least ten minutes ago, but she didn't want to leave the white noise and heat of the shower—because after her admissions and that panic attack, she really wasn't looking forward to seeing anyone. Embarrassment and shame made her cringe when she thought about her panicky freak-out and the fact that she'd shared what she'd promised herself she'd keep quiet. Now, she had no doubt that Sara was going to want to talk more. And she couldn't begin to imagine how she would face Easy.

"Yeah," she called as she wiped her hands over her face. "Be out in a minute."

Guilt cut through Jenna's belly. Sara had helped rescue her. Jenna *should* feel happy and relieved and grateful to be reunited with her sister. And she was.

Except.

She shivered despite the spray's warm temperature.

Being in Sara's presence reminded Jenna of what a freaking burden she was and all the ways that her illness—hell, her very existence—had hurt Sara over and over again.

Time to stop hiding. She turned off the water, grabbed the towel from the toilet seat, and dried herself off.

Then, almost holding her breath, Jenna did something she hadn't allowed herself to do when she'd come in the bathroom. She stepped in front of the mirror, lifted her eyes, and looked at her reflection.

"Oh, God," she said, as her gaze scanned over the black-and-blue ringing her right eye. She leaned in and tilted her face this way and that, getting a closer look. Everything between her eyelashes and eyebrow was purple, and the bruising extended above her eyebrow, too. A reddish purple beneath her eye extended to the side of her nose, where the bruising turned a sickly yellow. More purple colored her puffy cheekbone, where three little white strips held together a split right over the bone.

The hit to the mouth has bruised her, too. Not as bad as around the eye, to be sure. But the whole area below the corner of her lip was a reddish purple. Her gaze scanned downward to find that a bruise marred the skin at the top of her left breast and that purple fingerprints dotted her arms here and there.

Man, how she wished she could say, "You should see the other guy." Except, all her efforts to fight back had been absolutely useless. She tried to swallow around the lump in her throat.

"It's over," she whispered, bracing her hands against

the porcelain. As she inhaled a deep breath, her gaze settled on a pile of toothbrushes resting behind the faucet nozzles. What she wouldn't give to use one of them, but she didn't know to whom they belonged nor did she know anyone well enough to be at the borrowing-your-toothbrush stage. She brushed her teeth with her finger. Twice. And then she gave in to the urge to borrow the mouthwash sitting on the back of the toilet.

"I have some clothes for you," Sara said from the other side of the door.

Not wanting Sara to see any more than she already had, Jenna wrapped the white bath towel around her body like a cape, glad it was big enough to cover everything that needed covering. She glanced at her own clothes, which she'd stuffed into the plastic garbage can under the sink, then opened the door and found her sister standing right on the other side, her expression somewhere between hopeful and worried. The sweats and tee in Sara's hands didn't look familiar, which brought home the realization that Jenna had none of her belongings here. And neither did Sara. "Thanks. Where did you get this stuff?" Jenna asked, taking the items into her hands, which was a bit challenging with her arms under the towel. But Jenna didn't want Sara to see all the bruises.

"Becca," Sara said. "Do you remember her? You met her last night, but you were really out of it."

Frowning, Jenna tried to remember seeing anyone but Easy, but couldn't. "No, I don't think so."

"Well, you can meet her today when you're ready. She lives here, too. She's a nurse, and she's really nice. Luckily, she had some extra stuff we can borrow until we get ours."

Lives here, too? As in, what? They lived here now? "Why did you say it like that? 'Lives here, *too*.'"

Sara rubbed her forehead. "Well, just that, we'll be staying here now. At least for a while."

Jenna's thoughts were suddenly in a whirl. About how their lives had changed so quickly. About the fact that they were still in danger. About their father, who had left them in this mess in the first place. He'd apparently been involved with and indebted to the Church Gang before he'd died in a prison fight, which in the gang's estimation dropped the debt into Sara's hands to pay off.

"But all our stuff . . ." Jenna's belly squeezed as realization set in. "My books. Your sewing machine. Our pictures. What . . ." She shook her head, knowing it was stupid to worry about things like this given what she'd survived, but whenever life got hard, books were what had gotten Jenna through. When their dad went to prison, then died a couple of weeks later, when she had a bad seizure that knocked her down for a few days, when she and Sara fought—books helped her escape it all.

Now, she had absolutely nothing. Not even the clothes on her back since she planned to get rid of what she'd been wearing when she arrived.

"I know," Sara said. "And I'm sorry."

There Jenna went, making Sara feel bad again. She hugged the clothes to her chest. "Don't apologize. It's not your fault. But I'm confused. If Bruno's dead, why can't we just go back to the apartment?"

"Because Church isn't dead," Sara said, sadness slipping into her green eyes. "Dad's debt was to Church, so as long as he's alive, we're in danger. We're safe here, but our apartment's off-limits."

"If that's the case, what about moving to New York? I thought we wanted to get out of Baltimore altogether?" This was the plan they'd come up with a few mornings ago. The day after Jenna had learned about everything that had happened to Sara. And just a few hours before Bruno and his henchmen had broken into their apartment and dragged Jenna out. The only reason Jenna hadn't insisted they pack up and run that morning was because Sara had talked her into finishing out school for the semester so she didn't lose the credits.

Funny how, just a few days ago, college had been the most important thing in her life. All she'd wanted to do was get her degree and get out of their shithole apartment and start a life of her own. She'd been so dedicated to the idea that she'd taken summer classes every single summer so she could graduate early, leaving her with just a few classes remaining before she could get her degree. All of that felt like it belonged to a different person right now.

And all of it also felt incredibly selfish. Here she'd been focused on getting out and getting away, which would've left Sara in the middle of a horrible situation. All by herself.

Sara ducked her chin and hugged herself. "All the money I'd saved is still at the apartment. As are my truck and your car. We don't really have a way to go anywhere right now.

And I think Shane and the guys can help us here. I think . . . maybe we don't have to run away to be safe."

The mention of Shane's name resurrected Jenna's memory of the way Sara had looked at him. "So, you guys are serious?"

A quick nod. "Um, yeah. Crazy, huh?"

"I think it's awesome, Sara. You deserve it, and Shane seems like a great guy."

Sara's gaze flashed to hers, and the surprise on her face made Jenna feel like shit. Had Sara thought she'd disapprove? "You don't mind? I know we'd agreed to go—"

"Oh, my God, Sara. No. Of course I don't mind. And it's not like you need my blessing anyway. I only ever cared that you got free of Bruno and Confessions and that whole situation."

A silence stretched out between them until Jenna didn't know what else to say.

"Well, let me slip this stuff on, and I'll be right out." When Sara nodded, Jenna gently pushed the door shut. She forced a deep breath, then dropped the clothes to the toilet seat so she could hang up the towel. In between the tee and sweats in the pile was a pair of panties.

Jenna laughed. It totally took her by surprise, but once she started, she couldn't stop laughing. Because here she was in the middle of a situation where she had so little she had to borrow underwear, of all things. She laughed so hard, she had to brace herself on the sink. So hard, her lips and cheeks hurt, and she couldn't draw a full breath. So hard, her knees gave out, and she finally sank to the floor in a ball. Tears streamed down her face. She didn't even have her own underwear. Thank God she had small boobs and could get away without wearing a bra. That made her laugh even harder.

Clearly, she was cracked in the head.

When she could finally breathe and sit upright again, she took another look at those clothes. And didn't find them funny at all.

She forced herself to her feet again and mechanically pulled on each piece until she was fully dressed in a light blue T-shirt and dark gray sweats. The shirt was short-sleeved, baring quite a few fingerprint bruises. But what choice did she have?

Next to the bottle of mouthwash sat a man's toiletry bag. Given the brush that sat inside, she guessed that it didn't belong to Easy, so she hoped whoever it did belong to didn't mind her borrowing his stuff.

She pulled the brush through the dark red hair until she'd straightened all the tangles and it hung in long, damp threads almost to her breasts.

And then she was out of reasons to remain in the bathroom for even another minute.

But Sara wasn't in the hallway. Nor was she in Easy's room. And Jenna was kinda glad for the reprieve, especially when her gaze landed on Easy's duffel bag. Maybe he had a long-sleeved shirt that would cover up the bruises before Sara saw them. Or, oh, God, before Easy saw them. Before *anyone* saw them. Her face was bad enough, but unless she was willing to wear a bag on her head for the next two weeks, that much couldn't be helped.

Kneeling next to his bag, she carefully looked through

the neatly folded piles of clothing. His scent hung on the clothing, some tantalizing combination of laundry detergent, aftershave, and something masculine that was pure Easy. She felt kinda bad for snooping, but not as bad as she'd feel if she had to see everyone counting the number of marks she wore on her arms.

Nine. Depending on how you counted the ones that blurred together on her left wrist.

Toward the bottom, Jenna found a long-sleeved faded black shirt with the words "Pittsburgh Steelers" on the front in gold. It was the kind of worn soft that told you it was an old favorite. And her heart immediately latched onto wearing that one. Without allowing herself to think that through or second-guess her decision, she whipped off the blue tee and pulled on the black one.

It was so long the hem of it hung past her butt, and the sleeves had to be rolled twice before her hands would stick out. It was perfect.

And it made Jenna long for Easy's presence. His strength. His intensity. His touch.

"Hey," Sara said as she walked into the room. "I brought you a Sprite." She came to a halt just inside the door, and her gaze went to Jenna's shirt.

"I was cold," she blurted. "Do you think Easy will mind?"

Sara shook her head and sat on the edge of the bed. "I doubt it."

Jenna felt like she had to sit, too. She accepted the can of Sprite with a thanks and took a long sip as she sat down. God, the flavor and the fizz tasted so good.

"Hey, you might want to take that slower." Sara turned on the bed to face her.

"I know. I'm just really thirsty. And hungry, too. I'm not sure when I last ate. But I guess I better wait to see how this goes first." She took another long drink.

"Yeah," Sara said. And the air turned tense between them as Sara's expression crumpled. "I'm so sorry, Jenna," she said, covering her mouth. "I had one job, and I totally failed." Tears pooled and fell down her sister's cheek.

Guilt and shame tossed the soda in Jenna's stomach. "You have nothing to apologize for," Jenna said, sitting the can on the floor and scooting closer. Close enough that their knees touched. She grasped her sister's hands, which were shaky and cold.

"I do," Sara said in a tear-strained voice. "It's my fault that Bruno came after you. Because he was looking for me. He found out I'd been talking to Shane after I accidentally left a cell phone Shane gave me in Bruno's office. So stupid."

Jenna shook her head. "None of that matters. It's all just proof that Bruno was a controlling, possessive asshole." She leaned her forehead against Sara's. "Please don't think any of this was your fault. I've been enough of a burden to you without adding this to all the things you've had to deal with."

Sara sat ramrod straight. "You have *never, ever* been a burden to me."

Tilting her head, Jenna gave her a small smile though her throat went tight. "Come on. You were a nineteen-year-old college sophomore when Dad died, and you had to come home, drop out of college, and take care of me. And that's not even including all the stuff you had to do to be able to pay for my epilepsy meds and keep us safe. By any definition, that's a burden."

"I never felt that way about any of it, Jenna. And I'm so sorry if I've given you the impression that I see you that way."

"No, you haven't—"

"I have an idea," Sara said, squeezing her hand. "How about I promise not to blame myself for your k-kidnapping, and you promise not to ever think you were a burden to me."

Jenna stared at her sister a long minute, the words and the brightness in Sara's eyes luring her in.

"Clean slate, Jen."

Clean slate? The idea was tempting and scary and . . . exactly what they needed. She nodded. "Clean slate. I promise."

"I promise, too," Sara said, pulling Jenna into a hug.

They sat that way for a long time, and it was like a weight lifting off Jenna's chest.

"Do you want to talk about what happened? At Confessions, I mean?" Sara asked against her hair.

Jenna shook her head and pulled out of the hug. "No," she whispered.

"If anybody would understand, it would be me," Sara said hopefully.

Forcing herself to meet her sister's gaze, Jenna said, "I know. But I . . . I just . . . don't want to." She hated the flash of hurt and disappointment in Sara's eyes, but Jenna wasn't ready to put herself back in that place any more than she had to.

"Okay. Standing offer, though. Please know that."

"Of course." Out of nowhere, a wave of nausea washed through her. Jenna grasped her stomach and groaned. "Tummy is not happy with the soda, I think."

"Gonna be sick?"

"God, I hope not. Maybe I'll just rest." Jenna crawled toward the pillow. "Bring the bucket closer just in case?"

"Do you want me to stay?" Sara asked as she got off the bed, grabbed the bucket from across the room, and placed it next to the bed.

"No, that's okay. Go be with Shane," she said, enjoying the bit of pink that filled into Sara's cheeks. Jenna chuckled despite her rolling belly.

"I'll check on you in a bit," Sara said. On her way out, she flicked off the overhead light, leaving only the little lamp in the corner to throw off light.

It's not dark. Don't freak out. There's plenty of light. Right.

Jenna closed her eyes, thinking maybe she could sleep off the nausea. Problem was, when she closed her eyes, images she didn't want to see played on the insides of her eyelids. Bruno busting through her bedroom door. The gun in her face as she lay tied on the floor in the back of the van. The suffocating darkness of the black room.

Staring up at the men groping her while she lay helpless, unable to move a muscle.

Heart racing so loud it pounded blood behind her ears, her eyes blinked open, her gaze settling on the small lamp. A shiver passed over her body until she couldn't stop shaking.

And despite being rescued, Jenna couldn't help but wonder if she'd really ever be able to escape what had happened at Confessions.

Chapter 4

JENNA MADE IT maybe twenty-five minutes. Twenty-five minutes before she was nearly so terrified she was ready to scream for help.

As she flew off the bed, out of the room, and through the apartment, she hated herself for not being braver, for not being stronger, for not being tougher.

Her brain knew she was being irrational, but that didn't keep her imagination from conjuring every horrible scenario, her ears from hearing suspicious noises, and her heart from hammering like an attack was imminent.

Until she couldn't convince herself it wasn't true.

She only noticed the apartment enough to know she was alone. Racing down the stairs, she held tight to the gray metal railing, afraid in her shakiness that she'd go tumbling to the bottom. At the next landing were two gray doors, both with keypads next to them. Music sounded out from behind the one on the left, so she tried there. Locked. She knocked. Again. Then again. No answer.

She crossed the hall to the other door and knocked again. Nothing.

The shaking worsened. It was like a nightmare where you found one door after another but none would open.

Jenna started down the stairs again and found a door right at the bottom. More music played, but this one opened when she tried the handle, so she raced in.

She skidded into what looked like a lounge with couches grouped in one corner and a couple of tables and chairs filling the center. One wall had a large painting, almost like graffiti, that read, "Bleed with me and you will forever be my brother" in shades of reds and grays and blacks.

"Hello? Is anybody here?" she called.

Just then, a black-and-tan puppy came out of one of the rooms off the hallway in front of her and loped her way. The little thing was missing a leg, but its gait didn't seem too badly impacted by the loss.

"Hey, who are you?" came a woman's voice.

Jenna's gaze flashed up and landed on a petite woman standing in the hallway near one of the doorways. Dressed all in black, she had bright red highlights in her jet hair and tattoos all the way down both arms to her hands, currently covered by rubber gloves.

"I'm . . . J . . . Je . . ." She tried to swallow, but the panic was now gripping her throat. *Get a grip, Jenna!* But she couldn't.

"What's going on?" said a man as he stepped out of the

facing room. His gaze cut from the black-haired woman to her, and he smiled. "Hey, Jenna. How are you? Sorry, I had earbuds in. Jess, this is Jenna, Sara's sister," he said, walking toward her. And then his expression fell and he rushed over. "What's the matter? Are you okay?" he said, gently grasping her upper arms.

She flinched, not because she was scared of him—he seemed friendly enough—but because her central nervous system was on high alert. She couldn't help herself.

Next thing she knew, he took her by the hand and guided her to a couch. The little puppy followed and danced around their feet. They sat, the man never letting go of her hand, even as the puppy chewed one of his shoestrings. The guy fished his cell phone out of his jeans pocket. "I'll get your sister. Don't worry."

"No," she managed though it came out more as a moan. If Sara saw her like this again, she wouldn't be able to keep her promise not to blame herself. She wouldn't be able to *not* worry. And Jenna couldn't keep her own promise not to feel like a burden if Sara was upset over Jenna. What a mess.

"No? Not Sara?" he asked.

Jenna shook her head, but wasn't sure if he'd be able to tell with how bad she trembled.

"Hey, Jess? Can you grab that blanket from my room?" he called over his shoulder.

The woman appeared a moment later with a black-and-purple fleece, and the man took it from her and shook it out. "I guess I can forgive that Steelers shirt. Just this once." He winked, held up the Baltimore Ravens logo on the corner of the blanket, and wrapped it around her shoulders. Then he grasped her hand again.

"Th-th-thank you," she managed, as the warmth settled over her. Already, being around other people was helping take the worst edge off her panic.

"You're welcome. I'm Jeremy, by the way. Nick's brother. Oh, have you met Nick yet?"

"No," she whispered.

"Well, we'll get you introduced to everyone. Don't worry. Nick and I own this place," he said. "Welcome to Hard Ink Tattoo." Another wink, then he scooped the puppy into his arm. "And this little monster is Eileen." The puppy licked Jeremy's jaw, making him laugh.

He was so friendly that a smile tugged at the corner of Jenna's lips. She nodded, then she heaved a deep breath. "E-Easy?"

Jeremy tilted his head. "Easy? You want E?"

Jenna gave a fast nod.

"I think he's up in the gym. Think you can walk?" He placed the puppy on the floor and shooed her away.

"Yeah." But when they stood, the room went a little wobbly around her. If she could just get in a deep breath . . .

"Whoa," Jeremy said, catching her by the shoulders. "Maybe you should wait here, and I'll—"

"No," she rushed out. "I c-can do it." She closed her eyes, pictured Easy's face from before, and forced a couple of not-deep-enough breaths. When she felt less shaky, she gave a nod.

"If it's all the same to you, I'd like to keep ahold of

you on the steps so you don't lose your balance. Would that be all right?" He peered down so he could see in her eyes. And now that the panic was easing off, Jenna could take in just how cute Jeremy was. Disheveled, dark brown hair, pale green eyes, piercings on his lip and eyebrow, and lots and lots of ink.

"'Kay." As they made their way back out of Hard Ink and up the steps, Jeremy kept up a steady stream of chatter, and though Jenna couldn't really follow the names of all the people he was talking about, his presence was calming and distracting. Before she knew it, he was punching a code into a keypad outside the door she'd knocked on before, the one with the music, and they stepped inside.

The room was huge. All cement floors, brick walls, and exposed beams, and filled with tons of gym equipment.

And there was Easy. Pounding out a fast run on a treadmill.

Jeremy guided her closer.

Easy's feet sounded out a steady *thump-thump* as they hit the surface, but what Jenna most noticed was that he was shirtless. And every bit as cut as she'd imagined earlier. His shoulders bunched, and his back muscles rippled as his thick arms pumped. A pair of workout pants hung dangerously low on his hips, highlighting how narrow his waist was compared to his chest and shoulders. Beautiful, athletic, strong.

Jenna could already take a deeper breath.

"Easy?" Jeremy called over the music. "Hey, E?"

Looking over his shoulder, Easy's dark eyes went wide.

He immediately grasped the hand rests and jumped so that his feet straddled the moving belt, then he powered down the machine. "What's up?" he asked, his gaze focused on Jenna's face the whole time.

She tried to keep her eyes on his face, she really did. But as he grabbed a towel, turned, and walked toward her, she couldn't help but drink in the incredible definition of his chest and stomach. *Fit* didn't begin to describe this guy. He was . . . perfect. Gorgeous. Especially with sweat making his dark skin glisten. Not to mention the tattoo of a cross on a chain that went around his neck and down his chest and another with arrows and a dagger on his biceps.

"Uh, Jenna . . . needs you," Jeremy said.

Heat roared into her cheeks. He wasn't wrong, but his words combined with her current thoughts beckoned the reaction.

Easy frowned and came right up to her. "Thanks, Jeremy. I have this," he said in a deep voice.

"Welcome," Jeremy said. "You ever need me, now you know where to find me. Anytime. Okay?" he said to her.

"Okay," she said, dragging her gaze away from Easy to give Jeremy a smile. "Thanks for this," she said, handing him his blanket and finally noticing the shirt that he wore. It had the words, "The Man," with an arrow pointing upward, following by, "The Legend," with an arrow pointing downward.

He grinned and winked when he saw her reading his

shirt. He gestured toward himself. "It's true, you know. Jus' sayin'."

"*Good-bye*, Jeremy," Easy said.

Jenna managed a breathy chuckle. "Thanks, Jeremy."

And then she was alone with Easy. His fingers settled on her chin and brought her gaze back to his face. "What's going on?" he asked, the intensity of his gaze a little hard to hold.

"It's kinda stupid," she said, feeling more and more self-conscious about her panic attack the more she calmed down.

His eyes narrowed. "Doubt that. Just tell me."

"I was trying to sleep in your room and I . . . got . . . um, scared." She looked down, though Easy's grasp wouldn't let her move her head away.

"Look at me, Jenna," he said. She did. "You got scared, and you . . . wanted me?"

Heat roared into her cheeks until they were on fire. This guy was probably cursing the day they'd ever met. They barely knew each other, yet Jenna couldn't stop depending on him. Like she had any right to do so. Like he'd want to be saddled with a woman who couldn't stop puking or crying or freaking out. She closed her eyes and nodded. "Yeah." She released a breath, and her shoulders sagged under the weight of her admission.

"*Look* at me, Jenna," he said again, more sternly this time.

Her eyelids popped back open. And found his brown eyes absolutely blazing back at her.

EASY'S HEART POUNDED in his chest. And it had absolutely nothing to do with the five miles he'd just run.

Jenna needed him.

Fierce protectiveness and a deep masculine satisfaction roared through him. She'd sought him out for comfort, for strength, for protection.

Not only that, she was wearing *his* shirt. And she'd been staring at his body like she was fucking hungry.

Needless to say, the past few minutes had tripped *all kinds* of switches in Easy's brain where Jenna Dean was concerned. But he had to dial himself down. She was scared. And hurt. And clearly traumatized by everything that'd happened.

He leaned down to look her in the eye, trying not to focus on the bruises—he didn't want to make her feel self-conscious, and he sure as hell didn't want to get any more enraged on her behalf than he already was. "You *ever* need me, for any reason, I am here for you. No questions asked. Got that?" He brushed his knuckles down her uninjured cheek.

"Yes," she said, giving him a quick nod and leaning into his touch. And damn if that didn't make him feel ten feet tall—a notable feat for a guy who'd felt beaten down for most of the past year.

He gently rubbed his hands over her arms. "What do you need right now?"

"I don't even know." Pretty blue eyes searched his. "I've been fighting nausea off and on, but I can't sleep because I get scared when I'm alone. I'm hungry, but I'm afraid to eat anything. And I don't want Sara to know any of this because I don't want to upset her." Her gaze flickered off to her right, and Easy looked that way to find Marz and Charlie sitting at the desk in the corner, working but occasionally glancing their way.

"That's Marz and Charlie. Would you like to meet them?"

She ducked her face, and with that one gesture Easy knew she wasn't ready for people to see her like this. Bruised and shaken and scared. And he found himself wishing he'd been the one to kill Bruno all over again.

"How 'bout we wait for the intros 'til you're feeling a little better?" he asked. The relief that filled her expression reached into his chest and squeezed his heart.

"Yeah. Thanks."

He focused on what she'd said, and wondered which of her concerns he might be able to address. She needed sleep, food, security. Hell, he could handle all of that, if she'd let him. And, damn, feeling not only needed but useful? It was like hitting the damn jackpot.

"Do you think you could sleep if you weren't alone?" he asked.

Her eyes went wide, and he saw the answer on her face before she even replied. And it filled his gut with all kinds of *Hell, yes.*

"Maybe," she finally said.

Maybe, his ass. But he played it cool even though his mind was truly trippin' over how good it felt to be needed.

"Come on, then." He folded her little hand inside his much bigger one and guided her toward the door. Walking next to her emphasized how small she was compared to him. Her head just reached his shoulder. The disparity made him feel that much more protective of her.

They took the steps slowly, and Easy couldn't help but draw satisfaction from the fact that her trembles had almost completely died away. But he didn't let that fool him into thinking she was okay. She'd had two panic attacks within a few hours' time. It seemed he wasn't the only one very likely rockin' some PTSD.

Of all the things to find in common with this woman, he really wished that weren't among them.

And here they were stuck in the middle of a situation in which it would be hard to get her the help she needed. Wasn't like they could just run all over Baltimore. Not with Church very likely looking for Sara and Jenna, not to mention their rescuers. Rock, meet hard place. Fuck you very much.

Inside the apartment, Easy led Jenna to his bedroom, where the little lamp on the floor was still lit. "Would you be okay if I took a quick shower? I won't if you'd rather—"

"No, of course it's okay," she rushed out, her gaze dragging down his chest again. Just like she'd done in the gym.

Easy swallowed hard and willed his body not to react. But, damn, it had been a long time since a woman had looked at him the way Jenna was doing now. Way he'd been feeling, it'd been a damn long time since he'd even put himself out there. Turned out being pretty well convinced you were a worthless piece of shit responsible for the death of your best friend didn't put you in the dating frame of mind. Go figure.

Annnd that thought quickly doused any arousal Jenna's gaze had been stirring.

"Okay, then. Be right back," he said. When she nodded and smiled, he left for the bathroom, shut the door, and ditched his clothes. He'd taken some fast showers in his day. Hell, during basic, they'd had three minutes to get in and out of the shower all while their drill sergeant hovered over them with a stopwatch. This shower was on par with those.

Last thing he wanted was for Jenna to get scared again. Not on his watch.

Except . . . all he'd been thinking about was getting back to Jenna as quickly as possible. Which meant he *hadn't* been thinking about what he planned to wear when he returned to his room. Where she sat waiting. For him.

As he dried off and stepped out of the shower, Easy's gaze snagged on a wad of clothing stuffed into the small plastic trash can under the sink. He knelt . . . and pulled out the Lenny Kravitz T-shirt Jenna had been wearing when they'd rescued her. Dropping his forehead to the fabric in his hands, Easy's gut squeezed as he remembered the day he'd thrown away the bloodied clothing he'd worn during the ambush. He'd discarded it not because it'd been stained but because he'd never again be able to look at it and not remember how the blood got there in the first place.

Carefully, gently, Easy folded the shirt into a neat rectangle and returned it where he found it—where Jenna had discarded it . . . in favor of one of his shirts.

The thought hauled him off the floor. He wrapped the white towel around his waist. No choice but to brazen it out.

He stopped in the bedroom doorway and eyeballed his duffel. He didn't want to freak her out by parading around half-naked, but there was no help for it. Jenna sat perched on the corner of the bed, one foot bouncing in agitation, her hands fisted in the comforter. Damn, talk about brazening it out. She was scared. He'd put money on it. And so focused on just making it until he returned that she hadn't even noticed him.

He cleared his throat. "You okay?"

Her gaze flew to where he stood, and then she did a double take. "Uh, yeah," she said. He didn't miss her quick face-to-feet sweep of his body, nor the fact that her foot stopped shaking.

"Sorry, I was so focused on being fast that I forgot to take clothes."

"Oh, no worries," she said, dropping her gaze to the floor.

Easy crossed to his bag and crouched to grab a few things. He'd spent a lot of years in the Army honing his survival instincts. Like most elite operators, he had a knack for knowing when he was being watched. And those instincts were roaring right now. Heat flooded through his blood. He wasn't sure what it was about Jenna, but she'd made him feel more like a man in the past few days than he'd felt in the whole last year combined.

"I'm sorry I borrowed your shirt without asking." Her voice was quiet, uncertain.

And he was having none of it. Clothes in hand, he rose

and turned, grabbing onto the towel at his waist so it didn't fall. "Not even a thing, Jenna. You need something and I have it to give, I will, every damn time. You hear me?"

He wasn't sure whether he was more intrigued by the smile that played around her lips or the way her cheeks turned pink. "Yeah," she said.

He nodded and gestured to the hall. "Be right back." Just before he walked out the door, he glanced over his shoulder, and found her gripping the bed and bouncing her foot again. Because he was leaving.

Then he wouldn't leave. At least, not enough to actually leave her alone. "All right, Jenna. I'm getting dressed right outside the door. Don't come out now. Wouldn't want to tarnish my reputation."

A soft chuckle floated out to him. "Riiight. Okay." But he heard the relief in her voice, too, and that was all he needed to know he'd made the right call. He dropped the towel and nearly jumped into his clothes, one eye on the bedroom doorway, one eye on the apartment doorway. He'd never live this down if Marz or Beckett walked through the door right now. Not likely, since Marz was neck deep in research, and Beckett had run out to buy more burn phones, but when was the last time things had gone his way?

When you met Jenna?

Easy froze just as his fingers grasped his zipper, then he slowly pulled it up. Hell, yes, when he'd met Jenna.

"Okay, I'm decent," he said, returning to the room. He hung the wet towel on the inside doorknob. "Want this open or closed?"

"Closed." Her gaze was full of blatant interest as it ran over him again, and it felt like a physical caress despite the jeans and white undershirt.

"You got it." The door clicked shut.

Jenna scrubbed her hands over her thighs. Another nervous gesture.

You didn't spend eight years in the Special Forces without also learning how to read people. Which was part of the reason Easy was so pissed at himself over Marcus's death. Because the morning their convoy had been ambushed at a roadblock that had no business being where it was, Colonel Merritt had been jingling something in his pocket. Later, Easy had asked him a question, and the Colonel had been staring off into space and hadn't heard him. Neither the nervous tick nor the distractedness was typical of Frank Merritt, yet Easy had explained them away. And three hours later, six of their friends were dead, as well as Merritt himself.

Hindsight was a fucking bitch.

But none of that mattered right now, did it?

Easy knelt in front of Jenna, determined to get to the bottom of her nervousness. "Okay, what will most put you at ease? Because you are wound as tight as a top."

"I know. My thoughts are just all a whirl, and I—"

Easy caught her gesturing hands in his. "Not a criticism. Just an observation. And I want to help."

A series of emotions flashed over her face. "Why are you being so nice to me?"

"Truth?" Easy asked, wondering just how much of it she needed from him to be more at ease.

"Please," she said in a small voice, her gaze dropping to a point somewhere between them.

"Look at me, Jenna," he whispered, loving her eyes on him, loving her *seeing* him when he'd felt like such a ghost for so long. When she lifted her face, Easy let the truth fly. "Because I like you. And you deserve to be treated with kindness. And it feels good to be needed."

It was the first real smile he'd seen her give since they'd rescued her. And for the first time, he felt something that might actually be hope.

Chapter 5

"CAN YOU LIE down with me? Maybe just until I fall asleep?" Jenna asked. "I know it's stupid—"

Easy put his fingers on her lips, and damn were they soft. "Shh. I don't want to hear you apply that word to yourself one more time. Got me?"

"I just feel like I should be stronger than this," she said as she grasped and squeezed his hand, then continued to hold it.

Hell if Easy didn't know *exactly* how that felt. How many times had he berated himself for not being stronger? How many times had he been so weak he contemplated just giving up altogether? On himself. On the world around him. On life itself.

Didn't get any weaker than that.

And, Jesus, if he'd given in to those dark thoughts and even darker imaginings, he wouldn't be here right now. He wouldn't have been here to rescue Jenna from a fate maybe even worse than death. He wouldn't have been here when she needed him.

And that was the moment when Easy understood what people meant when they described suicide as selfish.

Looking down, he watched Jenna slide her slender white fingers between his thicker black ones, interlacing their hands. He fucking loved the way her skin looked against his.

"Trust me when I tell you I understand that. Completely. But sometimes," he said as he peered into her eyes again, "sometimes you gotta let someone else help you be strong before you can stand on your own." The words resonated inside him, shining light on a whole lotta truths he was going to have to face. Wasn't he.

Jenna nodded, and Easy pulled her to her feet. He tugged down the covers and gestured for her to get in. She chose the side that would allow her to lie on the uninjured side of her face.

"After what you've been through, I don't want to do anything that makes you feel uncomfortable," Easy said.

Propping herself on an elbow, Jenna shook her head. "You won't. You're the—" She blanched as if she hadn't meant to say whatever she'd nearly said.

Which made Easy need to know. He crawled on the bed as if lured by the words. "Finish. That. Sentence."

She eased back onto the pillow, red hair sprawling around her shoulders like silk, and stared up at him. And it took everything Easy had not to settle himself on top of her and tease the words out with his hands and tongue.

"The only one who makes me feel safe," she whispered.

Satisfaction humming through him, Easy turned and stretched out on his back. Because if he kept looking at her while she was looking at him like that, he might not be able to restrain himself from having what he wanted. A taste. A chance.

None of which she was in any shape for. And given the shitstorm in his head, probably neither was he.

"Good. That's good," he murmured, blowing out a long breath. Damn, he was tired. Not just because he hadn't slept much the night before. But because of the size of the load he'd been shouldering for the past twelve-plus months. If he could only figure out how to put it down. He scrubbed his hands over his face, wishing he could shake himself out of this fucking slump.

If Rimes were here, he'd kick Easy's ass for being such a morose motherfucker.

But he wasn't here. Which was the damn problem in a nutshell.

He dropped his arms to the bed and peered over at Jenna.

She lay on her side facing him, hand tucked under her chin, not looking the least bit settled or relaxed.

"Whatchu need?"

"You." She spoke the word without any hesitation, any doubt, any seeming self-consciousness.

"Have me, Jenna. Whatever you want," he said, his cock stirring no matter how hard he reined himself in.

Holding his gaze, she moved closer until her head rested on his shoulder and her body trapped his arm between them. And, suddenly, she wasn't fucking close enough.

"Here," he whispered, lifting his arm and inviting her closer. And damn if his heart didn't soar when she fitted herself the rest of the way against him, her face against his throat, her breasts against his ribs, her leg curling up onto his thigh.

He wasn't sure whose sigh was louder. All Easy knew was that this was the first time in more than a year he hadn't felt alone. Wrapping his arm around her, he couldn't resist squeezing her in just a little closer.

"Thank you," she whispered, her breath ticklish against his neck.

He laced his fingers between hers where they rested on his chest. "I gotchu. You just close your eyes and know I'm here."

JENNA AWOKE WITH the immediate realization that she was wrapped so tightly around Easy that she might as well have been lying on him. But she couldn't bring herself to feel bad or guilty or embarrassed about it in the least. Because his heat and his touch and his clean scent in her nose had allowed her to sleep without nightmares. And because she refused to regret something she wanted and might not get to have again.

After all, he'd said he liked her, but she had no idea exactly *how* he liked her. Maybe he meant like a kid sister. Or maybe he meant as a friend.

Except . . . his hips shifted under her leg, and she did *not* think she was imagining what she was feeling. He was hard. He was holding her, and he was hard.

Jenna's heart tripped into a sprint. Not out of fear but out of curiosity, amazement, interest.

Turning twenty in a little over a week, Jenna had had a few boyfriends. Despite her illness and living at home with her big sister, she wasn't totally inexperienced. But she'd never had sex. She'd thought that was where her and her last boyfriend had been headed, but then they'd cooled off and agreed to be friends instead. At the time, Jenna had been relieved.

And now she was lying in bed with an older man— how much older she wasn't sure—who made her feel safer than she'd ever felt in her life.

He was hard. She was more than a little intrigued.

Because Easy was patient and kind, and he made her feel special and cared for. And from his handsome face to his incredible muscles to the ink on his chest, he was totally, freaking gorgeous.

And he'd saved her life.

Couldn't forget that.

The simple act of thinking about the man in these terms made Jenna's belly flip.

And while she half expected to freak out at the idea of sex after she'd been pawed by Bruno's assholes, when she looked at Easy, she didn't see any of that, she didn't feel it, she didn't think about it.

What she thought about instead was that, if those assholes had killed her, she would've died without ever knowing what it felt like to love a man. And be loved in return.

She could've *died*.

The realization made her feel like she'd never really been living. But now she could. Now she had a second chance.

Jenna shifted herself closer, her body reacting to her thoughts and her closeness to his.

A hand clamped down on her thigh.

And Jenna's heart turned into a hammer inside her chest.

"Jenna," Easy said, voice full of gravel and warning.

She tilted her face upward, bringing her lips against his throat. And before she'd even thought about it, she kissed him. A long, soft press of her lips against the suddenly jumping pulse in his throat.

He groaned, and it was a sound as sexy as it was tortured. Beneath her thigh, he hardened further.

She kissed him again, dizziness threatening as her body slingshotted from sleepy to utterly, eagerly awake. And aroused.

"Jenna," he said again, though this time it came out as more of a plea. His hand slid up her thigh. His fingers pressed into her back, pulling her tighter against him.

She slipped her fingers from his and gently cupped the other side of his neck as her lips found his skin again and again.

Though she couldn't believe she was actually doing this, she didn't want to stop. And though he seemed to be trying to restrain himself, he wasn't stopping her, either.

Shifting closer brought his hip firmly between her legs. Jenna moaned at the friction against her center.

"Fuuuck," he rasped.

Jenna kissed the spot just below his ear, then his jaw, then she pushed up enough to make eye contact. And the heat and desire in his dark brown eyes nearly stole her breath.

Easy looked like he wanted to devour her.

And damn did she want to be devoured.

Her lips hovered so close to his that she could feel his breath caressing her. Staring into his eyes, she got closer, and a little closer yet, and then her lips brushed his.

On a groan, he hauled her body on top of his, letting her feel every long, hard inch of him. She'd thought she understood his power and strength before? It was nothing compared to feeling him move beneath her and hold her. Because the guy was all lean, hard muscle and leashed, lethal power. Yet he touched her gently, tenderly, as if he were afraid of breaking her.

Their kisses were soft, slow, almost tentative, and he let her lead even as his hands landed in her hair.

Need vibrated through her, and she licked at his top lip and shifted her hips against his length. One of his hands clamped down on her ass, holding her still yet pressing her more firmly against him.

"What are you doing to me?" he rasped.

"I just . . . need you," she whispered against his lips. God, how she wished the one corner of her mouth didn't sting because she wanted him so much that she just wanted to let herself go. But these slow kisses were good, too, because they allowed her to taste him, to learn him, to explore him.

"You feel like a fucking dream," he said.

The words as sweet as they were sexy, Jenna's heart squeezed and her blood heated even more. Their tongues touched and twined, and Easy lifted his head from the pillow to pursue her lips in return. Soft, teasing brushes and pulls and sucks at her skin that made her gasp and pant.

Cradling her by the head and the back, he gently rolled them over, his handing tangling in her hair, his chest falling on hers, his thigh pressing maddeningly between her legs. He kissed her uninjured cheek, her jaw, her throat. Jenna tilted her face away, giving him access—and ready to give him everything he wanted to take.

His hand fell on her hip and squeezed, and his touch so close to where she vibrated and grew damp with need made her moan and thrust her center against his thigh.

"Easy," she rasped.

He brought his face back to hers and kissed her full on the mouth.

A sharp sting on the corner of her lip. She sucked in a breath and flinched.

He reared back like she'd slapped him. "Jesus, Jenna. I'm sorry." And then he rolled away until he sat on the edge of the bed, his back to her and his face in his hands. "What the fuck am I doing?"

Jenna pushed herself into a sitting position and wrapped her arms around her knees, her body torn between arousal and confusion. "I don't want to stop," she managed to say as she rested the side of her face on her arms.

He shook his head and shifted to look at her, his expression stone cold pissed. "I shouldn't have kissed you—"

"You didn't kiss me. I kissed you." Part of her felt like she should be scared to push him, and there was no question that the expression he wore was freaking intimidating. But she also knew the sweet, protective man was in there. And that he'd wanted her.

I. Could. Have. Died.

And now she wanted to live. Now she wanted Easy.

She crawled closer to him, close enough that she could feel his heat but shy of touching him. "I still want to kiss you," she whispered, meeting his intense brown eyes.

"It's not right, Jenna," he said. His gaze drifted from her eyes to the side of her face. The side with all the bruises.

She touched her fingertips to the puffiness on her cheek. "Is it that ugly?"

His mouth dropped open, and he grasped her hand. "Hell, no. You are beautiful." The compliment gave her stomach the feeling of floating inside her. "Those bruises aren't ugly. They've proof that you survived. But they're also proof that you're hurt, and you've been through something traumatic." His brows cranked down, and he shook his head, like he was having an argument with himself.

Jenna nodded and looked down to their joined hands where they rested on Easy's knee. His thumb stroked over her skin again and again, and it was so comforting. She wondered if he even realized he was doing it. "I know all that's true, but it all feels better when I'm with you." She swallowed hard, then met his gaze. "And I don't mean that like I'm using you to forget. Please don't think that. It's just . . ." She shrugged and searched for the words.

Easy leaned his forehead against hers. "What?"

"I like you," she whispered. "And when I'm with you, I feel safe enough to just be a girl who likes a guy and not a kidnapping victim who could've died."

"Jenna—"

"Plus you're really sweet."

Easy chuckled. "Don't tell anyone that. You'll ruin my rep."

Jenna couldn't help but smile. He was even sexier with a little humor shaping his face.

Just then, Jenna's stomach growled so loud it was almost a roar.

"Saved by the stomach," he said with a wink.

She smirked. "Like you needed to be saved from me?"

"No," he said with a pointed look. "*You* needed to be saved from me."

Heat rolled over Jenna body. "But what if—"

He kissed her, just a soft press of his lips against hers that cut off her words. "A man can only resist so much temptation, babe. So whatever you were about to say, please don't." He winked, taking the edge off the rejection. "You're hungry, and I bet it's been a damn long time since you last ate anything. So let's take care of that need now. How's your stomach feeling?"

"Better," she said. And it did. The nausea was gone, replaced by an aching hunger that was almost painful. Easy was right, as much as she hated to admit it. "I guess I am hungry."

Easy smiled and sat back, his thumb still stroking over her hand. "You wanna come downstairs to grab some food? Sometimes we all eat together, and sometimes everyone fends for themselves. Not sure what the plan was today, but you could meet everyone, and I could show you around."

Meet everyone. As in, see all Easy's friends. Looking like this. She did want to see the guys again and meet those she hadn't met yet. And she especially wanted to thank everyone. But . . . it just felt like a lot.

"Or I could bring something up here and we could keep it low-key for tonight," he said, his gaze running over her face like he was studying her.

The idea couldn't have been more perfect. "I think I'd prefer that for tonight. I just feel a little shaky or something." She shrugged.

"Whatever you need," he said, his expression softening. "What do you like?"

"Anything really," she said with a smile. Because this big, strong, man was going to make her dinner. Could he *be* any more perfect? "I'm having the weirdest craving for a milk shake." She laughed. "There's a diner not far from our apartment that made the absolute *best* chocolate milk shakes. The kind where you get the extra can of shake along with the fancy glass." That thought led her to another. "Guess it'll be a while before I go there again, huh?"

"The truth?" he asked. She nodded. "Yeah. But it won't be forever."

She dropped her gaze to their joined hands again, a weird sadness suddenly flooding her. Everything was gone. Everything had changed.

Easy didn't let her hide though. He grasped her chin in his fingers and lifted her face until their eyes met. "It won't be forever. I promise."

Chapter 6

SON OF A *good goddamn holy motherfuck.*

That was the tenor of Easy's thoughts as he jogged down the stairs in search of dinner for him and Jenna.

What had he just let happen? And why the hell had he stopped it?

Actually, he knew the answer to the second one. Because it hadn't been right. Because Jenna had *just* suffered capture and abuse at the hands of kidnappers. Because she was too . . . too . . . everything. Too injured. Too young. Too innocent. For him.

She was sweet and kind and trusting. How could he *ever* saddle her with all of his shit? The guilt, the shame, the depression. Even worse? The hopelessness, the despair, the thoughts that maybe he should just end it fucking all.

Except . . . he'd been awake for a half hour, and this was the first time his typical negativity had filtered into his thoughts. When he'd been with Jenna, his head hadn't gone there at all. Not once.

Oh, he'd been mad at himself all right. He should've put an end to the kissing as soon as it started. He'd lain down with her to protect her, to give her a sense of security, to make her feel safe. And, if he was being honest, because it felt damn good to be needed, too. But no part of his agreement to get into that bed with her had ever even flirted with the idea of making a move on her. Not that he didn't *want* to touch her—he did. Since the night they'd met, her sass and her smile and her curves had intrigued him and lured him in. But Easy wanted a lot of impossible things—Rimes and the rest of the guys to be alive, Marz to still have his leg, all of them to still have their lives and careers. Being with Jenna was just another item on that impossible list. Par for the course, with him.

Nor had he ever expected her to make a move on him. She could've hit him over the head with a frying pan, and he would've been less surprised than when her lips traced along his throat.

But now that they'd gone there, Easy couldn't get Jenna out of his head. The feel of her soft curves against all his hardness. The taste of her tentative kisses. The sounds of her throaty little gasps and pleasure-filled moans.

Jesus. He could *live* on what she'd given him and die a happy man.

I don't want to die.

The thought took him by the throat and froze his feet to the floor.

He was so deep into his own head that he didn't even

notice the Rixeys' apartment door opening right in front of him until it nearly smacked him in the face. He caught the edge of it with his hands and reared back.

"Damn, sorry, man," Nick said, as he walked out onto the landing, his brother Jeremy right behind him. Two pair of pale green eyes settled on him, and he could almost hear the questions rattling around in their brains.

"My fault," Easy said, throat still tight.

Nick clapped him on the shoulder. "How's Jenna doing? Shane said you hung out with her last night so Becca could get some sleep. Appreciate that."

"Yeah, well," Easy said, shrugging and trying to put his thoughts into some kind of order. "Doing better. She thinks maybe she can finally eat, so I was coming down to see what I could scrounge up."

"I heard about the drugs they forced on her. Fucking scum bastards." A scowl on his face, Nick crossed his arms. Easy couldn't have agreed with him more. Damn it felt good to have someone understand so fundamentally where he was at, how he felt. Easy didn't have that at home. Not with the way he butted heads with his father—and always had.

You haven't told Nick everything about how you're feeling though, have you?

No, he hadn't. And the longer this mission went on and the more dangerous it got, the more problematic the lie of omission became. A key factor in keeping everyone on a team alive was understanding and compensating for each team member's weaknesses. But the guys had no damn idea just how weak Easy was.

"Wait, what?" Jeremy said, yanking Easy from his thoughts. Jer looked between them. "They forced her to take drugs? No wonder she was so hyped-up this morning."

Nick frowned. "What'd I miss?"

Easy scrubbed a hand over his hair. "Jenna's had a couple of panic attacks. She's okay, but she gets anxious when she's alone. Speaking of which, I want Sara to go hang with her while I find some chow."

"Last bedroom on the right," Nick said with a smirk. "Might want to knock first."

Jeremy rolled his eyes. "Dude, you are so not one to talk right now."

Straight-faced, Nick popped Jeremy in the arm with a fist.

"*Dude*," Jeremy said, rubbing his arm. "Maybe you aren't doing it right 'cause sex is supposed to chill your ass out."

Easy managed a smile. "I really like your brother, Rix," Easy said, looking at Nick.

Throwing an arm around Easy's shoulders, Jeremy grinned. "You have good taste in friends, Nick. Gotta give you that much."

A hint of a smile playing around his lips, Nick pointed at Easy, then Jeremy. "Fuck you. And fuck you." And then he crossed the hall and punched a code into the keypad next to the gym door.

"Aw, don't be that way, bro," Jer said. Nick flipped him the bird over his shoulder, making Jeremy laugh. "Annnnd such an easy mark."

"Amazing how easily you get under his skin," Easy

said. "I've always thought of Nick as letting everything just roll on off."

"I have special powers. It's coded into my DNA." Jeremy waggled his eyebrows. "Seriously, is Jenna okay?"

"She will be. Thanks for helping her before." Easy thought about all the ways that Jeremy had stepped up the past few days where the Dean sisters were concerned. First by extending them an open invitation to live in this building when he'd learned how Sara had been abused by the Church Gang. And second by putting the building up for collateral with the Raven Riders in case they hadn't nabbed the guns or there weren't enough of them to pay the MC off after last night's ops. Finally, by helping Jenna this morning. And those were just the most recent examples. Easy held up his hand, and Jeremy clasped it. "Thanks for everything you've done since we invaded your space. Above and beyond."

"Just wanna help any way I can," Jeremy said, and Easy could see the depth of the sentiment in the guy's eyes.

"Roger that. Okay, lemme go find Sara."

"Good luck," Jer said, starting down the steps to the tattoo shop.

Inside the Rixeys' apartment, Easy went straight back to Shane and Sara's room and knocked.

"Come in," Shane called from inside.

Easy cracked open the door and peered in. Shane and Sara were stretched out side by side on the bed looking at a laptop screen.

"Hey, E? What's up?" Shane asked.

Easy looked from Shane to Sara, suddenly a little un-comfortable. Because he'd spent most of the day asleep with Jenna. It hadn't occurred to him to wonder what Jenna's sister would think of that until this very moment. "Uh, I came down to get Jenna some dinner, and I won-dered if Sara would go hang with her. She's still a little shook-up."

Sara was off the bed before he'd even finished asking. "Of course," she said, and it was clear she was *dying* to help. Boy, did Easy understand that. She came up to him in the doorway and placed a hand on his chest, allowing him to register that Sara was taller than Jenna. "Thank you for taking such good care of her, Easy. It seems like you two have some kind of connection and, well, I'm happy she has someone who's making her feel better through all this." Sara pushed onto her tiptoes and kissed his cheek.

And that was the second time a Dean woman had taken him by surprise today.

Not exactly sure how to respond, Easy nodded. "I'm happy to do it."

"I'm glad," she said. Looking over her shoulder at Shane, she said, "I'll be back in a bit."

Shane winked. "Take your time, sweetness."

When Sara left, Easy said, "Sorry to interrupt," then he tapped the doorframe with his hand and made to leave.

Shane closed the laptop and got up. "Jenna needs any-thing twenty-four/seven, just ask. It's not an interruption. I feel almost as protective of her as I do Sara," he said, raking his hand through his hair.

"Yeah," Easy said, wondering whether Shane intended any secondary meaning to his statement. Easy headed for the kitchen. Shane followed and took up a perch on a stool at the breakfast bar as Easy poked his head in the fridge. Looking at food made him realize he was nearly starving and, unlike Jenna, he'd eaten breakfast. After a few more minutes of foraging, he settled on chicken soup and a plain toasted bagel for Jenna and a roast beef sandwich for himself. "Think this is okay?" Easy asked. "You can't imagine how many times she threw up. I don't wanna make her sick again."

Shane surveyed everything Easy laid out and nodded. "Bland is good. She really needs to get back on the anti-epileptics tomorrow. Getting some food into her will help her system soak up whatever they gave her."

Easy threw the bagel in the toaster and dumped the soup into a bowl for the microwave. Just the thought of what had been done to her filled his head with a red-hot rage. Little as she was, they could've easily overdosed her. And from what Easy understood, Bruno fucking knew she was on meds, so he would've had to know there could be drug-interaction implications and not cared. Christ, they could've killed her.

And then he would've never seen her again, never held her, never received her kiss. Damn, it might be twelve kinds of wrong, but he wanted all of that. He wanted more.

Blowing out a breath, Easy stretched his neck. No sense in getting himself all spun up before he went back upstairs.

Another thought popped into mind—thankfully, this one wasn't at all angsty. The milk shake she'd fantasized about having. Not bland, but if even a small taste made her happy, it would be worth it.

Opening the freezer, Easy smiled. God bless the Rixeys' ice-cream addiction. There were so many containers, it seemed entirely plausible that they'd robbed an ice-cream delivery truck. He sorted through the tubs until he found a container of chocolate.

Bingo.

Next, he grabbed the milk from the fridge. And then he opened a bunch of cabinets until he found a blender at the back of one of them. The layer of dust on its surfaces told of how long it had gone unused. He rinsed and wiped it off, then brought the detachable pitcher to the other counter, where the ice cream lay waiting.

Shane's expression was two seconds away from amused.

"Not a word, McCallan."

He held up his hands and shook his head, but he couldn't hold back the smile. Fucker.

Scoop, scoop, scoop, milk. Lid on, Easy placed the container on the blender and hit *mix*. Two minutes later, he had something approximating a very thick milk shake. He spooned it into a glass, then gathered the bagel and soup. Next he built his sandwich, sneaking pieces of beef and cheese as he worked.

"Damn, that looks good," Shane said, pushing off the stool and grabbing a plate for himself. "Think I'll make some food for me and Sara, too."

Easy suddenly felt less self-conscious with Shane making food for his woman, too.

Whoa. He froze with a piece of rye bread in his hand. Jenna was *not* his woman.

But maybe she could be.

Slapping the bread on top of the lettuce, Easy's thoughts spun—he came up with lots of reasons why it probably wasn't a good idea, but that didn't make him want to consider it any less. He sighed as he cleaned up his mess.

Mid-sandwich-making, Shane spoke in low, even tones. "We don't have to do that thing where I tell you to handle Jenna with care if you're thinking of starting something with her, do we?"

For. Fuck. Sake.

Not that Easy was particularly surprised by the question. Hadn't he been half expecting it? And, his brain noted with interest, it wasn't a warning off.

"Nope."

"I didn't think so," Shane said in that same casual, even tone. "I see how protective you are of her, Easy, and I'm glad for that. I know you'll treat her right. But you should know that her birthday's next week."

Easy's gaze flashed to Shane's. "And this is relevant how?"

"She'll be twenty."

Easy had to grab the counter. "Say again?"

Twenty? Jesus, he'd known he was older, but he had a full decade on her.

"You heard me." Shane sucked a bit of mustard off

his finger. "Sara's only twenty-three, so I'm not saying a thing about it, except handle with care."

Nodding, Easy concentrated on making the floor stand still under his feet. Twenty. He blew out a long breath. "I like her, Shane," he finally said, echoing the conversation he and Shane had had a few nights ago about Shane's growing feelings for Sara. And, well, *hi, how ya doin', Mr. Hypocrite*, Easy had told Shane he had to come clean with the team. Despite the fact that Easy hadn't done so himself. Still.

"Yeah," Shane said, clapping him on the back of the neck and squeezing. "I know."

Twenty. Wow.

Staring at the plates and cups he had to take upstairs, Easy shook the whirling thoughts away and recalled seeing exactly what he needed. From the thin cabinet next to the oven, he retrieved a baking sheet to use as a tray. Improvisation he could do. He loaded it down with everything he thought they'd need and lifted it into his arms.

"She not ready to be around everyone yet?" Shane asked.

Easy paused and looked his friend in the eye. Shane McCallan was a good guy through and through, and the fact he implicitly understood where Jenna was at right now meant a lot. "No. The bruises are filling in pretty good. I think she's feeling self-conscious. She'll come around, though."

Shane nodded. "All right. Tell Sara I made us something to eat?"

"Yup," Easy said, and then he was all about getting back to Jenna.

JENNA SMILED WHEN Easy walked into the bedroom, carrying what appeared to be half the refrigerator on a bowing cookie sheet. Not only had he made and delivered dinner, he'd sent Sara up to keep her company. How much more thoughtful could he be?

He glanced between her and Sara like he was unsure what to do next. Jenna pulled the covers back so the surface would be flat and patted the bed next to her. "Put it anywhere."

Easy set the makeshift tray down and rubbed a hand over his head. "I tried to think of things that would be gentle on your stomach," he said in a low voice. "But if you want something different—"

"No, this looks perfect." Her gaze settled on a tall glass of . . . She gasped. "You made me a milk shake?"

At that, Sara patted her on the knee. "Okay, I'm gonna go. Let me know if you need anything?"

"Oh, uh, Shane was making you all something to eat," Easy said.

Sara smiled. "Good timing. This is making me hungry," she said, gesturing to the tray.

Jenna grabbed up the milk shake and hugged the glass against her chest. "Get your own."

Holding up her hands in surrender, Sara smiled. "All yours. Besides, Nick and Jeremy have the world's biggest sweet tooths. There's an endless supply of ice cream downstairs. I'm not even joking. So there's more where that came from." She squeezed Easy's arm. "You know where to find me if you need me," she said.

And then they were alone.

Jenna was glad. Not because having Easy here warded off her panic and fear but because she just wanted to be with him.

She fished a spoon out from between two plates and took a taste of her treat. Freaking heaven. "Oh, my God," she said, scooping another big bite. "This is *so good*. I can't believe you made me a milk shake." Even when her father had been alive, Sara was the one who'd really taken care of Jenna. So maybe Easy's thoughtfulness wouldn't have been so earthshaking to someone else, but to her, it meant a lot. She peered up at him, which made her realize he was still standing. Crisscrossing her legs, she pointed at the foot of the bed. "Come sit down. Some of this has to be for you, too, right?"

"Yeah," Easy said. "You sure this is okay?"

"It's great, really. I can't even remember the last time I ate, so this is like filet mignon and Maine lobster rolled into one. Seriously." She exchanged the milk shake for the bowl of soup, and the warm, salty broth tasted every bit as good.

They ate in silence for a while, then he asked, "So, what are you studying in school?"

"International business," Jenna said around a spoonful of soup. "I always wanted to travel." And, to put it more plainly, she'd always wanted to get the hell out of *here*. Which made her break her promise to Sara—it was really hard not to feel bad about wanting to leave Sara knowing everything she'd been going through. Jenna was going to be a work in progress on that, it seemed.

"Sounds ambitious," Easy said. "Did you have to learn languages?"

Jenna nodded. "I minored in Spanish, and I've taken some French, too. What I'd really like to learn is Chinese since there are so many new markets opening up there. But I've heard it's really hard. Do you speak any other languages?"

Wiping his mouth with a napkin, Easy nodded. *"Hablo español, árabe, y Dari."*

Grinning, Jenna reached for her bagel. She'd thought him hard to resist just being his usual sexy, thoughtful, protective self. If he was going to throw speaking to her in a foreign language into the mix, she'd be a goner. "What is Dari?"

"One of the main languages in Afghanistan," he said.

"Oh. Guess that makes sense. Are Arabic and Dari hard to learn?"

"Yeah. Where I grew up in Philly, there were a lot of Hispanic kids, so Spanish was like a second language. But coming to languages as an adult about kicked my ass. Cultural training is a big part of Special Forces training, though. We're not out there just trying to win battles, but hearts and minds, too. So . . ." He frowned. "Or, we were, anyway."

"Sounds like you liked it," she said, unsure why he seemed suddenly sad.

"It was the best thing I've ever done." He put down

the sandwich half he'd been holding and brushed off his fingers.

Jenna was suddenly filled with the certainty she needed to tread carefully. "So, why did you get out?"

He tilted his head and stared at her. "Sara didn't tell you?"

"No. But you don't have to talk about it if you don't want to."

"You're in the middle of it now, Jenna, so you deserve to know." He took a long drink from a bottle of water, drawing Jenna's eyes to the way his throat worked as he swallowed, which made her remember how that very skin had felt against her lips. Soft. Warm.

She blinked out of the memory and focused on what he'd said. She was in the middle of it? Of what?

Easy lowered the bottle and played with the cap for a minute. "Remember how Sara said we were running an investigation?" When Jenna nodded, he continued, "Me and my guys, we were discharged from the Special Forces about a year ago. The five of us were the only survivors of an ambush, and we were blamed for the rest of the team's deaths."

Jenna's mouth dropped open, and her stomach fell in sympathy.

"We *didn't* do anything wrong," he said with a whole lotta edge in his tone. "Turns out our commanding officer was involved in some sorta criminal activity on the side. We didn't know about it, but after he died, someone arranged for a cover-up that hung us out to dry. Trying to get to the bottom of all that? That's what we're investigating."

Jenna dropped the last of her bagel to the tray. "I'm so sorry, Easy. About your team. About what happened to you and the other guys. All of it. That's so unfair."

His lips pressed into a tight line. "Yeah."

"How did that lead you to Baltimore and the Church Gang, though?" she asked, thoughts whirling.

"Some of that's still unclear. Our commander's kids live here, and the Churchmen came after them looking for information related to their father. Two weeks ago, Charlie went missing, and his sister Becca came and found Nick, who was our team's second-in-command, here at Hard Ink. After we rescued Charlie, he told us he'd found a number of links between his father and the Churchmen. We're guessing it has something to do with the heroin trade, which would paint a pretty direct line between Afghanistan and a gang like Church's. But that's about as much as we know. It's a fucking mess."

She reached across the space that separated them and grasped his hand. "I'm sorry," she whispered, her chest aching for him, aching for the hurt and anger she could see in his eyes and his expression.

He looked her in the eyes. "You shouldn't be the one apologizing, not when our bullshit ended up hurting you."

"Easy, what happened to me wasn't your fault. It was my father's fault for getting involved with Church and not protecting me and Sara from the fallout." And she wasn't sure she could ever forgive him for that, either.

"Still, I'm really fucking sorry for what happened to you, Jenna. I wish . . . if I'd stayed with you . . ." He shook his head.

She squeezed his hand. "Hey, don't torture yourself. You can't ever know if a 'what if' is actually how things would've happened. You got me back. That's all that matters."

"Well, I'm kind of an expert in torturing myself." He shrugged, and his expression was so sad it nearly broke her heart. "You're a good person, Jenna Dean."

"So are you," she said.

A storm rolled in across his expression. "No, I'm not. I was, but . . ." His hand fisted around his napkin.

Jenna's stomach twisted at the pain radiating off him. What would make him say such a thing? She pushed the tray out of the way and scooted closer, needing him to know, to believe. Taking his face in her hands, she forced him to look at her. "If it wasn't for you, I wouldn't be here right now."

"My team would've gotten you. It wasn't just me," he said, voice like gravel.

"But it was you, too. And you got rid of Confessions, right? That was all you. You'll never know what a relief it is to know Sara will never have to go there again." Jenna's throat went tight. Slowly, carefully, she threaded her arms around his neck and hugged him. Under her touch, his muscles were rigid, bunched, braced. But then it was like he melted, and his arms came around her in return.

For a long moment, he held on tight, like she was his anchor in a storm. He was certainly hers. And then he pulled back enough to rest his forehead on her shoulder, the pain that had rolled off of him moments before replaced by a heavy weariness. She stroked the back of his head and neck, soft caresses meant to comfort. She loved holding this big man in her arms, loved knowing that maybe she wasn't the only one in need of some comfort and protection and reassurance.

"Know what'll make you feel better?" she said after a little while.

"You?"

Her heart literally panged in her chest at the sweetness of that single word. She kissed the side of his head, his super short hair tickling her lips. "Besides me." Reaching out with her hand, she grabbed the milk-shake glass and her spoon. Easy sat up, an eyebrow arched as he looked between her and the ice cream. She scooped some onto the spoon and held it out to him. "Trust me."

Skepticism plain on his face, he ate what she offered.

Jenna couldn't keep from grinning at his lack of reaction. "You clearly need more. Here."

He swallowed the second spoonful, too, but still wasn't looking particularly better.

"This is a very serious case," she said, playfulness plain in her tone. "Better make it a double this time." The spoon nearly overflowed.

A smile played around the corners of Easy's lips, and it filled her chest with a warm pressure. He ate it just before it dripped, humor creeping into his dark brown eyes.

"See? It's working. I knew it." She held the spoon out again.

This time, after he ate it, he stole the spoon right out of her fingers. "Problem is, you aren't administering this medicine the proper way," he said as he filled the spoon himself.

Jenna grinned again, happy to see some lightness returning to his expression. "I'm not?"

"Nope," he said, shaking his head. "This is what will really help." He held the spoon up to her lips.

"How will me taking it—"

"No questioning. Just obeying." There was that cocked eyebrow again.

"Oh, is that how it is?" she asked, smirking. When he just stared at her, she gave in and ate the ice cream.

Next thing she knew, his lips were on hers. The kiss was as gentle as it was thrilling—because Easy was the one initiating this time. After he'd pulled back earlier and said it hadn't been right, she wasn't sure what to expect from him. If anything. But this was sweet and filled with such tenderness that it made the back of her eyes prickle. Avoiding the cut on her lip, Easy's cool tongue slowly snaked over her lips and stroked at her tongue. He grasped the back of her head as he kissed and nibbled at her. The rich flavor of the chocolate combined with another taste that was all Easy and made her moan in appreciation. His grip tightened, his tongue stroked deeper, and a throaty groan spilled from his lips.

One more soft press of his lips against hers, and he pulled away.

Jenna was nearly panting, and very definitely wanting more. "You're right," she said panting, "that is much more effective."

He gave a rare, open smile, and it made her happy to see it after how sad he'd seemed a few minutes before. "Told ya," he said with a wink.

She nodded. "But, you know, that could've been a fluke. Just to be sure it really worked, maybe you should, um, give me another dose?"

Easy looked at her a long moment, then leaned in and scooped another spoonful from her nearly empty glass. He held it out to her, making her heart flutter in anticipation. When she tilted her head toward the spoon, he yanked it away and ate the ice cream himself.

"No fair," Jenna sputtered, reaching for the spoon. "That is not what the doctor prescribed."

Holding the spoon above his head put it out of Jenna's reach, even with them sitting on the bed. She pushed to her knees, grabbed hold of his shoulder, and lunged for it. Laughing, he banded an arm around her lower back and held her in place, easily avoiding her grabs.

Jenna couldn't stop laughing as they wrestled for the spoon. It was stupid and silly and childish . . . and exactly what she needed. And it seemed he did, too. It was perfect.

Wriggling out of his grasp she braced herself on his shoulders and tried to stand. Next thing she knew, he had her around the legs and took her down to the mattress in some sort of super-fast ninja move. She screamed and laughed, and he was laughing every bit as hard as he came down on top of her. And, oh God, his laughter was a sweet and sexy rumble that lit her up inside.

"You fight dirty, Easy," she said around her chuckles.

His grin faded, but the humor hung on the edges of his full lips. "I haven't had this much fun in so long."

She caressed his face with her fingers. "Me neither. Between overloading on classes and my epilepsy, I often feel like a little old lady trapped in the body of a twenty-year-old. All I need is some cats."

"Cats are kinda awesome," he said. "When I was a kid, I used to sneak stray cats into the house, just for a night or two. I'd keep them in my room and bring up bowls of milk and cans of tuna for them."

"Aw, you were a sweet little boy, weren't you?" she asked, loving how he was opening up to her. The closeness, the sharing, the way his big body was lying on her legs and hips, leading him to prop his head up on her lower stomach—both her heart and her body reacted.

"Maybe for about five minutes." He winked. "Mostly, I was a hell-raiser. Growing up, we didn't live in the best neighborhood. Drug dealers on the corner, gang activity trying to pull in even the younger kids, crack house one block over. All that. Trouble wasn't hard to find." He shrugged. "Army straightened me out, though."

"Well, we lived in a nice neighborhood growing up and here my father *was* the freaking drug dealer on the corner. Or close enough, anyway." Jenna stared at the ceiling and shook her head. "Sorry, I didn't mean to get serious."

His thumb stroked along her side, sliding the cotton of her borrowed shirt against her skin in a way that almost tickled. "Don't apologize. Our histories are what they are, you know?"

She nodded and gave him a little smile. "Yeah."

Shifting off her, Easy stretched out alongside her and propped his head up on his arm. "I'm thirty, Jenna," he said out of nowhere.

And he was telling her this because? He thought their age difference was too great? He thought she was too young? He was worried she would think he was too old? Probably D) all of the above. Thing was, all she saw when she looked at Easy was a guy she really freaking liked. One who'd saved her life, helped make her sister safe, and gave her a sense of security she hadn't felt in years. He was hot as hell, easy to talk to, and one of the kindest guys she'd ever known. Maybe some of that was *because* he was older. Who knew?

"And I need to know this because?" she asked, resting her head on her arm.

The muscles of his shoulders lifted into a shrug, but his face was contemplative. "Because there's clearly something going on between us."

Heat rushed across her body. There'd been plenty of evidence that the attraction wasn't all on her side, but hearing him admit it out loud made her heart flutter and race. She held up a hand, and he laced his fingers between hers. "When I look at you, I don't see a bunch of differences, Easy."

"What do you see then?"

Warmth flooded into Jenna's cheeks, and she chuckled. He'd said that she was beautiful, after all, so why couldn't she give him a compliment in return? "A really hot guy I'd like to get to know more."

A smug little smile slipped onto his face, and she might've rolled her eyes if it weren't so damn sexy. "*Really* hot, huh?"

"Well, kinda hot, anyway."

"Nuh-uh," he said, tugging her hand to his chest. "Can't take it back now."

Cheeks burning and big smile threatening, she rolled onto her side to face him.

They lay there, side by side, her chest almost touching his, looking at each other. Tension and desire and anticipation crackled in the space between them, unleashing a flock of butterflies in Jenna's stomach.

"What do you see when you look at me?" she whispered, half-afraid to ask but even more curious to hear what he'd say. Did he mostly see someone who was too young for him? Or a needy girl he'd had to save and babysit?

Easy squeezed her hand and tugged her closer. She sucked in a breath, sure he was going to kiss her. He did. Just not how she'd thought. His lips pressed to her forehead, then he pulled back to look her in the eye. "I see a woman who's made me feel more alive in the past few days than I have in a long, long time."

Chapter 7

As he looked into Jenna's eyes, Easy wasn't sure what the hell he was doing. Or, as the hours passed by, what the *right* thing even was.

Because he was well versed in all the reasons he should be backing off. Problem was, Jenna Dean soothed a very jagged part of his soul. Actually, that wasn't a problem at all.

She didn't heal what was broken within him—he wasn't that naïve or delusional. But she sure as fuck made him remember the man he'd once been. Made him see glimpses of that man within the person he was right now. And made him believe maybe he could become that man again. Hell, maybe he couldn't ever go back. But something about her smile and her touch and her belief in him made him believe, too.

No matter what, he could be a better man than he'd been this last run of months.

But he'd have to reach for it, work for it, fight for it.

And Jenna provided one helluva motivation.

Right now? He wasn't good enough for her. But maybe he could be.

"I think that's the sweetest thing anyone has ever said to me," she said, voice thick with emotion.

Easy leaned in—

Knock, knock.

His eyes locked with Jenna's, and they both gave a rueful smile and sat up.

"Come in," she called.

Sara and Becca walked through the door. "How are you?" Sara asked.

"Hey," Jenna said. "I'm okay."

Sara's gaze made a quick survey of the two of them. "Did you manage to eat something?"

Jenna tossed the napkin and placed the glass and spoon on the tray. "Yeah, and my stomach's feeling fine. Better now, actually." Easy was really glad to hear that because it probably meant whatever Bruno's thugs had given her was working its way out of her system.

"Good," Sara said, relief filling her expression. "Jenna, this is Becca."

Scooting to the edge of the bed, Jenna gave a little wave. "Hi," she said. "Sara said you helped me last night. Thank you."

"You're welcome. I'm just glad you're feeling better." Becca smiled and tucked her hair behind her ear. Despite his anger toward her father, Easy had liked Becca from the night he'd met her. She'd helped break up a fight between Nick and Beckett, cleaned up Nick's busted cheek, dressed them all down for their behavior, and earned Easy's respect all in one fell swoop. And then there was that day on the boat when she'd apologized for what happened to him and his team and promised to help clear their names. Her words had reached inside his chest and removed a weight from his heart—because she was the first person to ever apologize, to ever believe, to ever offer to stand beside them and try to right the wrong that had been done.

Where he came from, that meant a lot.

"I thought Becca should take a look at you and make sure everything's okay," Sara said, shifting on her feet.

Jenna held out her hands. "Uh, Sara, I'm fine." A pause as Jenna looked between the three of them, as if looking for backup. "Buuuut this will make you feel better, right?"

Sara chuckled and hugged herself. "I'm sorry, but you didn't make me promise not to worry."

With a big sigh, Jenna said, "Okay, but after this, you have to promise that, too."

"Deal," Sara said, smirking.

After seeing how much and how violently Jenna had been sick not all that many hours ago, Easy was sympathetic to Sara's worrying. "I'll clean up this stuff and give you all some privacy," he said, reaching for the tray. He put the water bottles on the floor for later but gathered up everything else.

"Thanks for getting dinner for us, Easy," Jenna said. She looked at him with such gratitude and affection that it both set off a warm pressure in his chest and made him self-conscious—because he was acutely aware that Sara was observing them. She had to know that something was going on. Given how little he thought of himself sometimes, it wasn't a big leap to imagine others would think the same. Just because Sara had seemed appreciative that he'd helped Jenna didn't mean she'd approve of anything more, especially after everything Jenna had been through.

"You know, you set off a milk-shake-making party," Becca said.

Sara laughed. "Yeah. Shane made us shakes, then we took them over to the gym, and Nick was all jealous he didn't have one."

Grinning, Becca rolled her eyes. "Which was hilarious because he didn't even know they owned a blender."

Easy stood. "Well, I guess I'm glad I could provide such a valuable service." He winked and looked at Jenna. "Need anything else while I'm downstairs?"

Smiling, she shook her head. "Don't think so, but thanks."

Easy made his way out of the room, through the night-darkened apartment, and back down to the Rixeys', where he found all the guys in front of the big flat-screen TV—Nick and Marz kicking back in the recliners, Beckett and Shane sprawled on one couch, and Jeremy and Charlie on the other, with Eileen between them. It was dark in the room except for the flickering light of the screen.

A round of greetings rose to meet him.

"Sexual Chocolate!" Marz yelled over the others.

Easy couldn't help but smile as his gaze settled on

the television, where the classic Eddie Murphy movie *Coming to America* was playing. One of Easy's all-time favorites. He placed the tray on the counter, then turned and held his hands out. "Good morning, my neighbors!" he said, mimicking one of the prince's lines.

Right on cue, Marz said in a thick New York accent, "Hey, fuck you!"

Easy could quote this movie *all day*. "Yes, yes! Fuck you, too!"

The guys all chuckled, and Easy leaned his butt against the arm of the couch next to Jeremy and got sucked into the movie.

"How's Jenna doing?" Shane asked after a few minutes.

Easy nodded. "A lot better. She slept, she ate. Seems like the nausea's over."

"Glad to hear it," Shane said, just as everyone burst out laughing at the movie.

Nick laced his hands behind his head. "Hey, wanted to let you know we got in touch with Louis Jackson. He's on board."

"Good," Easy said. Part of him felt a little bad that the rest of them had apparently gotten at least some work done while he'd slept all day. But another part said that Jenna had needed him, and that was every bit as important.

Something popped into mind, and Easy looked at Marz. "Did you get a chance to look at the chip?" Before they'd teamed up with the Ravens and gone to rescue Jenna and intercept the Churchmen's gun deal, they'd accidentally made a discovery—a tiny microchip hidden in the eye of a stuffed bear that Becca's father had sent her before he died. Just one more in a long string of mysteries and questions.

Marz gestured to Charlie. "We worked on it for a while, but when we hit the stage of wanting to throw our computers out the window, we took a break. There are so many fucking layers of encryption and password protection on this thing, it ain't funny."

Charlie crossed his arms. "We'll get it, though."

"Believe it," Marz said. "If either of us had access to our regular setups, we'd probably already have it. We did go through the pictures Sara took of Bruno's files, though."

Easy's gut tightened. Sara had taken that risk trying to help the team, but it had inadvertently set off a chain of events that led to Jenna's kidnapping after Sara's thug boyfriend realized what she'd done. "And?" he asked.

"The files on Charlie and Becca were both dossiers compiling information on jobs, associated addresses, and known routines. Pretty clearly part of the Churchmen's plans to grab them. The Nunya file—gangbanger-speak for "none of your business," I'm guessing—listed illegal business deals going back several months. It appears Church routinely bought heroin using girls and cash, then sold the heroin to raise coin and buy guns. No details on who the trading partners were, though." Marz waved a hand. "We'll figure it out."

"I don't doubt it," Easy said, nodding to Charlie. "I'm just glad you have some help now." Marz had been handling 90 percent of their research on his own, but since his rescue, Charlie had rolled up his sleeves and become integral to the team on all things computer.

The movie played on, and the women didn't return, so Easy figured they were hanging out. Jeremy and Charlie made room for him, but as Easy sat there, two competing thought streams interrupted his ability to just relax. First, how damn good it felt to be with the guys. Not working, not stressed, not under fire. Just kicking back and shooting the shit.

Which was quickly followed by the whole muddied stream of thoughts that said Easy was an asshole for not fessing up about how fucked his head had been. Still was.

Say something. Just do it now. Everyone's here. We have the time. Just open your mouth.

His adrenaline spiked at the thought of saying the words that needed saying. His stomach squeezed. He realized he was bouncing his foot.

Fuck. He was a ball of anxiety.

All the more proof he needed to spill. Before his bullshit got someone hurt. Only way *that* would be acceptable was if it was him.

No. No more of that.

Shit.

Easy's gaze settled on Shane as the credits rolled. Shane knew something was up. He'd asked a few times, most pointedly this morning. And the guy had medical training. Maybe Easy could practice this opening-himself-up crap with just one of them first.

Coward.

Yup.

Pulse spiking, Easy leaned forward, braced his elbows on his knees, and looked at Shane. "Can I talk to you a minute?" he asked, mouth dry, gut twisting.

"Of course." He arched a brow. "Uh, here or . . ."

Easy nodded toward the back hallway that led to Shane and Sara's room.

Shane was immediately on his feet. Easy didn't make any eye contact with the other guys as he got up and followed, but instinct said he had a whole lotta eyes on his back right now.

In the bedroom, Shane flicked on the light and closed the door. "What's up?"

Easy sat heavily on the edge of the bed and looked down at the floor. "Don't really know where to begin." Maybe he shouldn't do this. Having made the ask and dragged Shane back here, he had to say something.

Shane sat next to him. Hands clasped, he gave Easy a sideways glance. "Wherever you can. Wherever it's easiest."

He gave a rueful laugh. "Ain't no part of it easy," he said.

Shane didn't say anything, didn't push him, didn't rush him. Just sat there, providing constant, silent support.

Finally, Easy blew out a long breath and remembered how Jenna had made him feel as they'd talked before. And, really, who else in the world could he tell if not his teammates? Hell, you almost couldn't be a veteran without knowing at least one fellow vet who'd attempted or committed suicide these days. Sad fucking fact. He didn't want to put that kind of pain on his friends, not after everything they'd already been through.

Besides, how much longer could he slog through the shit this way? Right now, he was headed down a path he'd never thought he'd walk and he didn't want to travel anymore. Which meant it was time to ask for help.

"I have these thoughts sometimes." Even as his resolve to do this firmed up, his heart was a hammer against his sternum.

"Like what?" Shane said in a soft voice.

Easy swallowed hard, feeling like such a weak, fucking coward. "Like . . . that maybe . . . it would be better . . ." He shrugged. Giving voice to this was like performing a self-amputation. Messy, imprecise, and hurt like ever-livin' hell. " . . . if I wasn't here."

"By here, you're not talking about Hard Ink." A statement, not a question. So Shane was following him, then.

He shook his head. "Here as in, you know, uh, alive." His scalp prickled at the admission, and he forced himself to look at Shane.

The guy's face was a hundred percent rock solid. No pity, no sympathy, no disgust. But Easy saw the concern settle into his friend's gray eyes, and just that much of a reaction brought tears to his own eyes.

Lots of fast blinking to keep those motherfuckers from falling. He clenched his jaw so hard he gave himself a headache.

"Okay," Shane said. "Are these passing thoughts or are you thinking of ways to maybe make that happen?"

Easy had to wait a minute to respond, because he wasn't sure he could trust his voice not to crack. And damn if a single tear didn't escape. He scrubbed it away.

"Haven't tried anything," he said, wanting to make that much clear. "Mostly just general thoughts. Though, lately, some actual ideas have come to mind."

"Am I the first person you're talking to about this, E?" Shane asked.

Dropping his gaze to the floor, he nodded. His throat squeezed, his eyes throbbed with the pressure of threatening tears, his stomach twisted.

Shane's arm came around his shoulders.

And the reality of not being alone with the weight of these feelings crashed down on Easy. He lost it.

He lost it like his body was expelling a poison, hard and fast and violent.

Sobs ripped out of his chest. He slid off the edge of the bed and went into a balled-up sitting position on the floor. He buried his face in his arms and wrapped his hands around his head, just trying to hold himself the fuck together as he fell apart. Easy could've probably counted the number of times he'd cried in his life on one hand, and doing it now was about as comfortable as swallowing crushed glass.

Shane's embrace followed him to the floor, and was a constant, steady presence as wave after wave of grief rolled through him. Easy tried to hold them back, he really did. Every muscle in his back and abdomen ached from the effort to restrain the sobs, or at least to hold back the noise of his grief.

Adrift in a roiling sea of agony, time became meaningless. *I just want this to end, please let it end, please take all this away.*

He had no idea how long it went on, all he knew was that by the time he could manage a full breath again, he was damp with sweat and hot with embarrassment. At some point, he'd nearly curled into Shane's chest, or Shane had pulled him in. He couldn't begin to remember.

"Sorry," he croaked, voice like sandpaper.

"Nothing to apologize for," Shane said. And, whatdya know, his voice was full of the thin and tight, too.

Easy sat up, tugged at the hem of his shirt, and wiped his face on it. An odd lightness of being and an utter exhaustion fell over him like a wet blanket.

"I don't want to be a liability," Easy rasped, forehead in his hands. He heaved a shuddering breath.

"You could never be that, E. Don't you worry about a thing," he said, emotion bringing out Shane's Southern accent.

So completely wrung out that it took effort to lift his head, Easy forced himself to face Shane. That glassiness in the guy's eyes was damn hard to look at, but Easy appreciated it, too. Because it meant someone cared. It was proof Easy mattered.

"We are not losing you, too, brother. You are *not* going to be one of today's twenty-two. Nor tomorrow's. Nor any day's. That's a fucking promise," Shane said, nailing him with a glassy-eyed stare.

Twenty-two. Easy knew exactly what that number represented. The number of American vets who committed suicide. Every. Goddamned. Day.

"I need help," Easy whispered. Hard as it had been to say the words, the admission was like an exorcism—it left him feeling empty but more himself than he'd been in months.

"We're gonna work on that. I want you on an anti-depressant immediately. They take time to get into your system and start working, and sometimes it takes a little experimentation to find the one that works best. You need therapy, too, man. Just tellin' it straight. But the shit of the situation is that's gonna be hard for you to get right now. At least if you stay here."

Those words hung there for a minute, and Easy shook his head. "I'm not leaving."

"Easy—"

"Not just because of the mission, Shane. Part of me thinks that if I hadn't come . . . well, something mighta happened. I think Nick's call saved my life. How fucked-up is that?" He shuddered another breath.

"I don't think it's fucked-up at all. On some level, every one of us needed this. The reunion, the chance at redemption, some answers—all of it."

Blowing out a long breath, Easy forced his shoulders to relax and reclined his head against the mattress. "I'll take the meds," he said. "I'll try anything." Anything to be a better teammate and a better man—for himself, the guys, and Jenna. Sitting here now, he had to wonder why he hadn't done this sooner. Why he'd let the despair grow so dark and deep? The only thing he could think was that they'd reminded him of who he'd been and who he could be again. With help.

"This isn't the kind of thing that a family doc would normally call in a prescription for without seeing you first. Let me think about it, and we'll get that part squared away in the morning."

"'Kay."

"I hate to ask this, but do you have a weapon up in your room?"

Easy dragged his head upright again. "Of course."

"I'd feel better if you stored it in the gym," Shane said, regret clear in his eyes. "Depression plus opportunity plus weapons training equal up to the rampant suicide problem among vets. Add the kind of ingrained instinct not to fear pain that we had beat into us, and it's a recipe for disaster."

"Okay," he said again. He understood the logic, but it still stung. "I don't want to be benched, Shane. I've done my job this week. I didn't let it interfere."

Shane nodded and arched a brow. "I can agree to that as long as you're checking in with me regularly about where you are."

Another smack in the ass. But, whatever. "Fine."

Clapping him on the shoulder, Shane said, "Good man. Now, I want you to do one other thing for me. There's an assessment checklist that evaluates the presence and severity of PTSD. I'd like to have you fill it out. It'll give me a more quantitative baseline to work with."

"Yeah," Easy said. "Sure."

Shane shifted beside him. "I'm going to have to ask Nick or Marz to borrow a printer. So I need to know if the guys can know, or we're keeping this private."

Easy appreciated the option. He really fucking did. "I

think they gotta know." He shook his head. "I was worried you all might not understand. But now that I told you, I know that was the bullshit talking."

"Why wouldn't we understand, E?"

"'Cause you and Nick, and Marz and Beckett, you guys still have your best friends. And I—" A knot in his throat cut off the words.

"Aw, fuck. I miss Rimes, too. We all do. I get it, though. You guys came up and were together from the beginning."

Nodding, Easy tried to swallow. "And it was my fault," he rasped out.

Shane clasped a hand on the side of his neck and forced their eyes to meet. "How do you figure?"

"He was covering me. And then he got hit, and I couldn't get to him. When I finally could, he was already so far gone. I just watched him die. For me." The words flew out of his mouth, a rush of guilt and shame that had been eating at his soul for more than a year.

"Not your fault, Easy. Not any part of it. Was only by the grace of God that the five of us walked out of there. Actually, only two of us walked." The intensity of Shane's gaze willed him to believe.

The words *I didn't see any grace that day* perched on the tip of his tongue. But they weren't true, were they? Marz very probably should've died out on that road. When that grenade sheared off everything below his right knee, the blood loss was massive, and the shock was immediate. Yet he'd lived. And the shrapnel had very nearly taken out Beckett's eye, but he could still see. But, all this time, those weren't the things his mind had been able to recall.

Easy shook his head. "I don't know, man. My head hears what you're saying, but my heart . . ." He shook his head again.

"It's gonna be a process, but you're going to get through it. And I'm going to be there for you every step of the way." Shane squeezed his neck and sat back.

"Thank you," Easy said. "It's not enough, but it's all I got."

Shane smiled, a smaller version of his trademark crooked smile, the one that earned him guy friends and swooning ladies in equal measure. "It ain't even a thing. Now, how do you wanna do this with the guys? One by one, all at once, do you wanna wait—"

"Now," Easy said abruptly. "All of them."

"I'll see if they're still out there. If not, I'll round 'em up. Gimme five?" Shane rose to his feet, waited for Easy to nod, then walked out the door.

As the dim murmurs of voices from the living room reached him, Easy's stomach went topsy-turvy again. But it was less the terrified anxiety of before and more just the anticipation of getting it over with, so he could take the first step down the road to healing.

Years later, and not nearly long enough, Shane knocked softly at the door. "Ready?"

Easy went to push off the floor when Shane's hand appeared in his line of sight. Easy clasped hands with the guy and let himself be pulled up. And wasn't that the perfect fucking analogy for what was really happening here.

"You got this," Shane said. And then Easy followed him out to the living room.

Everybody was there, pretty much in the same seats as before except for Marz, who now sat by Beckett. But all the slouchy relaxation was gone. There was a tension in the air and in the guys' posture that said they knew something serious was up.

Easy braced his hands on the back of the empty recliner, Shane standing next to him.

Shane cleared his throat. "Do you want me to—"

"No. I gotta do this." One by one, Easy made eye contact. Nick, Marz, Beckett, then over to Jeremy, Charlie, and Becca, who'd returned from upstairs. They might not have been part of his Special Forces team, but they were a part of this now.

"What's up, E?" Nick asked, concern plain on his face and in his voice.

"I'm, uh, I'm in trouble," he said, palming the top of his head. Questions shaped everyone's expressions, and Easy knew he'd have to do better than that. He crossed his arms and focused on a point in the middle of the room. "I've been, um . . ." He licked his lips and shook his head. "Shit, I don't think I can do this." Restlessness suddenly crawled through his limbs, and he paced toward the door. When he turned, Nick was right there.

"This is just me and you," Nick said. "Whatever this is, I will have your back in a heartbeat."

Easy met the guy's pale green eyes and saw the truth

of his words. Silence rang loud in the room, and Easy was present enough in the situation to understand that what Nick offered was a proxy for talking to the group as a whole. Smart damn guy.

"Suicidal," Easy finally forced out. "Thoughts, mostly. A lot, actually. Some basic planning. No attempts."

Somehow, the silence got quieter, like Easy's words had deadened every bit of ambient noise, too. He couldn't even hear the sound of Nick's breath.

So everyone had heard him loud and clear.

Thank God.

Easy swallowed hard. "I should've said something sooner—"

Nick stepped closer and grasped Easy by the shoulders, and then he nailed him with a stare. "You are my brother as surely as if we shared the same blood, and I will help you beat this thing however I can. However long it takes. Whatever backup you need. I am *here.*"

Easy nodded. Marz and Beckett offered similar words of support, the latter of whom showed more raw emotion on his face than Easy had seen since the moment Beckett had learned about Marz's amputation. Jeremy and Charlie gave silent nods of support, and Becca a big hug and a whispered offer of help anytime. He appreciated every single expression of concern and support.

When it was all over, Easy felt like he'd humped a thirty-mile ruck march with a sixty-pound pack on his back. At least. But it was the absolute best kind of exhaustion, because it left him feeling free.

Chapter 8

IT WAS THREE o'clock in the morning, and Jenna couldn't sleep. She wasn't scared, at least not by the memories and images of her kidnapping. She and Sara had drifted off while talking—an old habit from way back—so she wasn't alone. And she was in her right mind enough so that her sister's presence here, Easy's presence somewhere nearby, and all the other Hard Ink guys being here, too, made her feel safe enough to slip into unconsciousness.

That wasn't the problem.

What was scaring her was that Easy had never returned. Not to check on her. Not to get ready for bed. Not for nothing.

Shane had come, though. To check on both Sara and Jenna. And something about him hadn't looked . . . right. Maybe it was the exhaustion on his face, or the way he seemed to regret parting from Sara, or the way his gaze didn't quite meet Jenna's.

Something was up.

Jenna's gut-deep certainty had her peeking at the time on the new phone Shane had apparently given Sara. Tiptoeing to the door, Jenna held her breath as she turned the knob.

"You okay?" came Sara's slurred voice.

Damn. "Can't sleep. You go back to sleep, though."

Rustling in the covers, as if her sister had sat up. "You sick again?"

"No," Jenna said. "Probably just screwed up from sleeping most of the day." Partially true, anyway.

But it wasn't all of it. Sara didn't need to know that, though, especially after the conversation they'd had about Easy—the one where Sara had urged Jenna not to rush into anything. Her concerns stemmed entirely from the fact that Jenna had been kidnapped, and Jenna got that. She did. But what'd happened to Jenna during her thirty-hour imprisonment hadn't been anything like the horrors of the almost-week Sara had spent in the basement of Confessions.

"I'm gonna go downstairs and watch some TV." Sara had made Jenna memorize the codes to the Rixeys' apartment and gym doors so she wouldn't ever be prevented from finding her in the building again. "Since you're awake, you can go back down with Shane if you want."

Feet hit the floor over by the bed, then Sara's phone lit up as if she were using it as a flashlight. "I don't want you to be alone."

"I won't be. Aren't there six people living in that apartment right now?"

Sara chuckled. "Yeah. It's like a college dorm."

"See? Come on, we can walk down together." Making sure she was decent in case they ran into anyone, Jenna tugged at the legs to the boxers she'd stolen from Easy's duffel, though his Steelers shirt was so long it covered them entirely.

They crept through the space, not wanting to wake the guys who apparently had rooms in the unfinished apartment, too. Downstairs, Sara had Jenna punch in the code to make sure she knew how the pad worked.

Even in the moonlight streaming in through high windows, the Rixeys' apartment showed off how awesome the upstairs would be when they finished it. High ceilings, red brick walls, and polished plank flooring extended in all directions.

"My door is the last one on the right, but are you sure you're sure?"

Jenna kissed Sara on the cheek. She'd been incredibly cool and supportive through all of this, worrying and all. "I'm sure that I'm sure that you're sure that I'm sure of being sure."

The darkness didn't hide Sara's smirk. "Good night, smart-ass."

"I love you, too," Jenna said.

Sara pulled her into a hug. "Me, too. Try to go back to sleep if you can."

"'Kay."

Moments later, a soft click down the hall told Jenna she was all alone. She padded over to the kitchen and opened the door to the fridge. A can of Sprite looked like nirvana, so she grabbed that and closed the door.

On the opposite side of the room, Jenna approached a wall of electronic components. So many little red and orange lights were illuminated that it could've been mission control. The moon highlighted the big rectangle of the flat screen and the red power button on the corner. Flickering blue light filled the space when she turned it on.

She cracked open her soda and searched the top of the shelf for the remote, then she turned to check the tables near the couches.

Jenna froze. Because Easy was lying asleep on the nearest couch. Stretched out, shirtless, and utterly gorgeous.

Should she stay? Should she go? Neither the light nor the sound seemed to be disturbing him, and her only other choice was to return to her room alone.

Which was all kinds of a no.

Besides, she didn't want to be anywhere else.

Decided, she curled up in the recliner nearest to the couch and surfed through the midnight underbelly of cable-TV programming. About once a minute—or at least it felt that way—her gaze drifted over to where the low light outlined the broad, inverted triangle of Easy's muscular back. Part of her yearned to lie down behind him, her body tight up against his, her arm around his stomach, her knees tucked up against his quads. Her skin could almost imagine the warmth of his just thinking about it.

She sighed. Why hadn't he come up to at least say good night?

Finally, she settled on a marathon of an old vampire series. She lay there so long, her eyes went bleary, and her left arm fell asleep. Unthinkingly, she shifted around to rest against her other side, which jarringly reminded her of the bruises on her face.

How she could've forgotten them, she didn't know, since now that she was thinking about them, they seemed to throb to the steady beat of her pulse. She ended up in sort of a contorted position with her head on the arm of the chair and her legs curled up against the back, but the pins and needles in her arm demanded the change.

And, nicely, however awkward the new position was, it offered the distinct advantage of giving her a clear view of Easy.

The next thing Jenna knew, she was floating.

She forced her heavy lids open and, sure enough, the ceiling moved above her. "What's happening?" she mumbled.

"Shh, just putting you to bed." Easy. Carrying her.

She put a hand on his chest and, lured by the warmth and the smooth expanse of hard skin, turned her face toward him. She breathed the masculine scent of him deep inside. "I missed you."

The next sensation that registered was the softness of the bed against her back. Her hands clutched his shoulders, not wanting him to go. But then she did. If he stayed, she wanted it to be because he chose it. Not because she asked, or pleaded, or because he felt a duty to do so.

Jenna wanted Easy. Simple as that. And she wanted him to want her in return.

His heat disappeared, and the bed shifted. Jenna's heart squeezed. He was leaving. Ah, well, guess that was her answer. Her mind was still playing that song when the bed shifted again.

"You awake?" he whispered.

"Yes?"

"Can I sleep with you, Jenna?"

Goose bumps erupted over her skin at the question. She knew he meant *sleep* sleep, but even that thrilled her. "I was hoping you would," she said.

He slid under the covers. They didn't touch. And the proximity without contact was *killing* her. Her mind became ultra aware, her skin almost tingly in anticipation of his touch, her body yearning to seek out his.

"Jenna, can I tell you something?" came his hushed voice in the darkness.

"Of course," she said, shifting a little closer.

"You may not like it," he said, an odd quality to his tone. Worry? Sadness? Fear?

"Okay." She couldn't imagine what he wanted to say, or what could've happened in the past few hours, but instinct insisted it was important.

The thick sound of a tortured swallow. "I talked to Shane and the guys tonight about something, and I want you to hear it from me." Jenna's heart tripped into a thumping beat that made her body vibrate. "I haven't been well, Jenna. Ever since everything that happened to us in Afghanistan. The friends we lost. Our careers ruined. Our reputation. It all weighs on me so much that some days it's a load I can barely carry."

Sadness and sympathy formed an aching pressure in her chest. Such terrible things had happened to him, and the injustice of it surely made it an especially bitter pill to swallow. "I don't blame you," she said. "It was horrible."

"It was. But what I'm saying is, sometimes I just wish I could escape it all. I think about that, Jenna. Sometimes even how I would do it."

The words hung there . . . . and slowly seeped into her brain.

She gasped. Was he saying . . . ? "Do you mean, like, hurting yourself? Or killing yourself?" Heart pounding and eyes stinging, she felt powerless and maybe more scared than she'd ever been in her life. For him. Arms screaming to hold him, she moved closer until her hands found his arm. His muscles went rigid, like he didn't want to be touched, so Jenna froze, not wanting to make him feel worse than he did.

He blew out a long, tired breath. "Yeah, that's what I mean. I told the guys because I need help. Medicine and maybe talking to somebody. We're gonna figure out a way to make that happen in the midst of all of this."

"Good," she said, wiping away a tear that spilled from the corner of her eye. "I'm so sorry, Easy. Have you been holding this inside all these months?" Imagining the loneliness of those feelings hurt her as surely as if someone had punched her in the stomach. When he didn't reply, she had her answer. "Well, I'm glad you told your friends. And me, too. How can I help?"

"What?" he asked.

"How can I help? What can I do to make this better?"

A long, tense silence she didn't understand, and then he said, "You . . . want to help?"

The doubt in those words pounded a raw ache through her veins. "Would you mind turning the lamp on, please? I'd really like to be able to see you."

When the golden glow illuminated the far corner, she found Easy standing there, not quite facing her and not coming close to making eye contact.

"Come back," she whispered. For a moment she thought he was going to question her, but then he stalked toward the bed and climbed back in. He lay down on his back pretty much as far away from her as he could and still be on the mattress. Fine. Then she'd go to him. "I'd like to hold you," she said. "Would that help, even a little?"

His head rolled toward her, and the low position of the lamp cast shadows across his dark face. "You heard what I said, right? You understand what I'm talking about?"

Jenna frowned. "Yeah. I get it."

He scrubbed his hands over his face, then crossed his arms tight over his chest. Everything about his body language radiated tension and defensiveness. When he didn't say anything, her brain whirled to make sense of what he was asking? Or, maybe even what he *wasn't* asking.

And the only thing she could come up with nearly broke her heart.

She grasped the bulge of his biceps. "Wait. Did you think if I knew this about you, I wouldn't want you?" Her memory resurrected his voice insisting he wasn't a good person, too. And the pieces of the puzzle started to fit together. He was hurting, unsure of himself, adrift in a sea of pain, clear from the tense set of his muscles and the lost expression on his face.

God. Here she'd been thinking about how *she* could've died. When, really, they *both* could've died. And never even had the chance to meet. Sadness weighed down on her shoulders at the thought.

Jenna fitted her body tight against the side of his, propping herself up on his shoulder so she could look into his eyes. "Easy, even if we are only ever friends, you will remain important to me for the rest of my life. You saved my life and Sara's life and gave us a chance at something real and free and safe. So if that's all we ever are to each other, I'd still want to help. I'd still want to hold you and ease your pain. I'd want to repay the way you saved me by saving you in return. If I could. That's not a question."

His eyes unshuttered, and his expression softened, like she was surprising him.

"But if you're as interested as I am in seeing what this thing between us might be, what you told me doesn't change my mind at all. It makes me care for you even more. It makes me want you even more. It makes my urge to help even stronger." Jenna stroked his face with her fingers and prayed she was getting through to him. "My situation was so different, of course, but I understand loss and betrayal. My father introduced me to the joys of those at the age of fifteen. Carrying that pain inside you doesn't make you any less of a person, Easy. Not in my eyes. Not in my heart."

Slowly, his big arms unfolded, one opening up to invite her in.

Relief flowing through her, Jenna eased herself against the crook of his body, laid her head on his chest, and wrapped her arms around him as far as they could go. His arms came around her in return, and they held each other like that for a long time.

Finally, she pushed up again so she could look at him and propped her head up on his chest. "I'm sorry you're going through this."

He nodded. "You really don't . . . think . . ."

She stroked her hand down his face. "What?"

"This makes me feel weak, cowardly, self-indulgent. I just didn't see how you could find me . . . attractive, given all this."

"Oh, Easy, I don't see a single one of those when I look at any part of you. And I will tell you every day until you believe me. You are the bravest, strongest person I know. And the fact that you're doing all this while you're feeling this way? Just proves it. Okay?"

He just looked at her.

She twisted her lips, returned the stare, and wondered how to convince him that she believed in him. "Repeat after me: I believe that Jenna believes in the good in me and always will. Your turn."

More staring.

She leaned in closer. "Come on, now. I believe that—"

"I believe that," he mumbled.

She gestured with her hands for him to continue, relieved that he was going along, however begrudgingly. "Jenna believes in the good in me and always will."

He sighed. "Jenna believes in the good."

"The good *in me* and always will. Come on. Almost done. Make ya feel better, I promise." And she needed to hear it, too. She needed to know he believed what she'd said and how she felt.

"The good in me," he murmured so quietly, she could barely hear it. "And always will."

"Not bad for a first time." She smiled and tried to keep her tone light even as her heart squeezed with emotion for him. "We'll keep practicing until you really believe it, too."

His smirk was miles better than the sadness and insecurity that had painted his handsome face moments before. "You're tough for being so little, you know that?"

"Hey, what can I say? Good things come in little packages."

His small chuckle seemed like such a victory. "Oh, baby, *that* I know for damn sure."

"You do, huh?" Jenna grinned as Easy nodded. Her playfulness was such a gift. So different from his norm, it drew him out of his usually distant shell. And his twisted thoughts.

The kind of thoughts that had kept his ass downstairs on the couch after he'd finished the PTSD checklist Shane gave him. After digging up all those feelings, giving voice to them, and seeing the quantitative proof of mental illness racking up as he marked a whole host of symptoms as occurring with moderate or greater frequency, Easy had gone straight to talking himself into believing Jenna would never want a man as weak as him. Or, more generously, that he shouldn't saddle someone like her with a guy like him.

"I was wrong to make assumptions about you," he said, looking up into her gaze. Her smile was full of warm compassion. "It was only because I was upset to lose the possibility of you."

"Here's the thing. Mostly, I'm doing okay right now with everything that happened. But I'm getting flashes of memories, and little bursts of physical anxiety for no apparent reason, and I'm jumping at every little sound—"

"Of course you are, Jenna. You're only two days out of being rescued from a kidnapping." Easy tucked a loose strand of red behind her ear.

"Exactly my point. We've both been through something kinda messed up. And we're both dealing with the consequences. Right?"

He stroked the soft skin on her arm with his fingertips, the small touches like a lifeline he couldn't resist. "Yeah."

Jenna tilted her head and gave him the sweetest smile. "Well, then let's do what feels good and figure out the rest as we go."

"I'm down with that," he said, stroking his fingers through her hair again. He loved the contrast of the silky red against the dark skin of his fingers and hands.

She leaned into the touch and closed her eyes, and the pleasure that shaped her beautiful face was its own fucking reward.

Having set loose all these emotions tonight, Easy was surprised his body had room for even one more. But there was no mistaking the arousal heating his blood and his skin where they touched, especially when she grasped his hand, brought it to her lips, and kissed his palm and the pads of each fingertip.

When she was done, she brought her mouth back to his middle finger and kissed there again. Except this time, the tip of his finger slipped between her wet lips.

Easy's cock jerked, and he rolled his hips, a reaction that was stronger the second time when her tongue snaked out and slowly licked up the length of his finger.

"Jenna," he said, his eyes glued on her mouth.

Her smile was pure seductive innocence as she dropped his hand and pressed her mouth to his bare chest. Small kisses and swipes of her tongue drew his hand to her hair. She flicked at his nipple.

Easy sucked in a breath, and his grip on her hair tightened as she pulled his nipple into her mouth. He let her tease and torment him for a minute, then he gently guided her upward. "Come here, babe."

He caressed just below the bruise on her chin. "Don't let me hurt you," he said, the thought truly sickening him, especially after the way she'd accepted everything he'd dreaded telling her with such grace, such open-mindedness.

"You won't," she said, her lips lingering close enough to his that he could feel her breath.

Easy kissed her. He stayed away from the cut, but he couldn't be as gentle as he thought he should, either.

Urges ran through his blood—to claim, to possess, to take, and they spilled into the way his lips sucked and pulled at hers, into the forcefulness of his tongue stroking against hers, into the tightness of his grip in her hair.

She moaned and gave every bit of it right back to him, making him feel claimed in return.

Exactly what he needed.

Holding her waist, Easy lifted her onto his body until her legs straddled his hips. Her weight fell on his chest and his cock. Both of them cried out at the first pressing contact. One hand kneading at her ass and encouraging her to rock against him, his other returned to her hair and guided the kisses he simply couldn't get enough of.

He hadn't been with a woman in over nine months, and he'd walked away from that last time feeling it had been a mistake. He hadn't been right in the head, and it had been with a girl from high school who'd still expected him to be his old self. The one that'd died on a dirt road in Afghanistan almost as surely as the men who'd never come home at all.

Efuckingnough. Just be in this moment. Have this. For once.

His hands roamed over her body, learning her curves and feeling her softness. He massaged her thighs, gripped her hips, and skimmed his fingers up her sides, slowly drawing the shirt—*his* shirt—upward. "Can I take this off, Jenna?"

A split second of hesitation, and she nodded. "Yes," she whispered. Together, they worked it over her head, Jenna guiding the neckline so it didn't hurt her face.

Holy hell, she was naked underneath. And gorgeous, with pale, creamy skin and small breasts just perfect for palming and sucking. He couldn't wait to get his mouth on her. On every part of her.

He pushed her into an upright position and moved his hands to her stomach. His gaze tripped on her sleep shorts long enough to realize that they were actually a pair of his boxers. And he'd thought the Steelers shirt had been sexy. Seeing her in his underwear was fucking insane. He plucked at the waistband. "I like this," he said, arching a brow at her.

She grinned and licked her bottom lip. "Me, too."

Easy chuckled, and his hands roamed higher. His dark skin was a stark contrast against her paleness, especially in the dim light of the small lamp, and it added another layer to his attraction and the wonder of being with her.

Easy released an appreciative *mmm* as his hands cupped her breasts, especially when her hands joined and tangled with his. Together, they massaged and stroked her as she quivered and rocked against his hard length. His body was already strung tight, and they'd barely touched each other.

He sat up and wrapped his arms around her lower back so he could hold her in place when he returned her earlier teasing. He kissed and licked all around the mound of her left breast. She cupped the back of his head in her hands, and he loved the feel of her caresses. When she whimpered and squirmed in his lap, he finally gave a long, slow, flat lick over the tight bud of her nipple.

He traced kisses to her other breast and started the

torment all over again. Something dark marked her skin. Easy pulled back thinking it was just a shadow, but it was a series of interconnected bruises. Not huge, not representing a physical injury of any real danger, but his gut dropped because he thought he knew exactly how she got it.

Her fingers slid over the bruise, luring his gaze to the skin of her arm. More bruises. Small. Round. Heat seared through his veins. Fingerprints. "It's okay. They don't hurt that much at all."

Gently, he pushed her hand away from covering her breast and pressed a barely there kiss over the mark. "It's not okay, Jenna. And it makes me need to ask: Are you sure you're okay with *this*?" he asked, the bruises like neon reminders of what she'd been through not that long ago.

"I'm completely sure. I want this." She grasped his neck and kissed him. "Tonight, I'm just a girl who likes a guy."

He studied her for a long moment and nodded, intent on giving her every ounce of pleasure he could. He returned to worshipping her, licking and sucking at her nipples, her neck, and back to her mouth again.

Jenna gasped and moaned, each sound sweeter than the last.

"I have to feel you under me," he said, lifting her off him and laying her out on the bed. She was a fucking dream to behold, all petite, feminine curves, red hair spilling all around her beautiful face and bright blue eyes staring up at him with such affection and desire.

To be wanted . . . sometimes that was every-damn-thing.

Easy crawled over Jenna, his knees straddling one of her sexy thighs, his hand braced at her shoulder. He gently cupped her throat, then dragged his hand in a slow sweep down her chest, between her breasts, her stomach.

Jenna lifted her head and watched right along with him. "Your skin is so freaking gorgeous, Easy. I love the way we look together."

"So do I," he said, his fingers tracing teasingly, almost tickling by the way she squirmed, along the waistband. A hot thrill shot through him, spiking his pulse and making him harder. He couldn't believe he was lucky enough to experience this with someone as good and beautiful as Jenna Dean.

"*I believe* . . ." Jenna's voice replayed in his memory from a short while ago and challenged his thoughts.

Okay, he did believe it. Because he was touching her and seeing her and hearing her little throaty gasps and moans. But that didn't mean he wasn't the luckiest so-nofabitch ever. Right in this moment, he most definitely was. And damn if thinking *that* didn't represent a pretty fucking major step forward for him.

He slipped just his fingertips below the waistband and raised his gaze up her body. "What do you want, Jenna? Tell me, and I'll give you anything."

Chapter 9

JENNA NEARLY SHOOK she was so filled with excitement and desire and amazement at getting to be with Easy. He was tender and intense, gentle and strong enough to move her bodily where he wanted her, and devouring and savoring by turns. She'd shared more emotion and intimacy with Easy in the last few days than she'd shared with some of the guys she'd dated for months. Sex had never felt right before because the guy had never been right before. Now, he was. And Jenna was absolutely ready to share her whole self with Easy.

"I want you, Easy. I want to be with you," she said, staring up into his blazing-hot gaze. Everything about the moment felt right to her, felt safe. And she was tired of waiting to live. Heart racing, she reached down and pushed his boxers and her panties over her hip bones.

"God, Jenna," he said, taking over. He dragged the cotton down her legs and tossed it somewhere behind him. And then she was totally bare to his hungry gaze. "So beautiful," he said, smoothing his hands up her thighs. His fingers skirted by her center without touching, but Jenna still gasped and moaned. He leaned down and pressed a kiss to her stomach, then pushed off the bed to stand beside it.

If Jenna had thought her heart flew before, it was nothing compared to watching this beautiful, muscular, tattooed man undress for her. The jeans slid over his lean hips and down his long legs, and he stepped out of them, but all Jenna could focus on was the incredible bulge filling out the front of a pair of black boxers. Easy wasn't the first naked guy she'd ever seen, but he was certainly the biggest guy, the most fit, and the oldest. Not that the age difference mattered to her—because it didn't—but his body had a more defined quality to it that she didn't recall seeing in guys her own age.

Easy was freaking gorgeous. No other way to put it.

She scooted closer to the edge of the bed and caressed his corded thigh with her fingers, softly, tentatively. She knew the things she wanted to do, but she wasn't sure what he might prefer.

His hand grasped hers. "Anything you want, baby," he said, bringing her hand over his erection. The groan Easy unleashed at her touch—still through the cotton—shot liquid heat through her body and made her wet between her legs. He was a big handful, long and thick in her fingers. A wet circle formed near his tip, and her gaze lifted up to his.

"Off," she said, grasping the band.

He nodded, and they worked them down to join his jeans.

Jenna's mouth dropped open at getting to see his cock. Skin a shade darker than his stomach stretched tightly over the erection, making him look like he was absolutely aching. She took him into her hand and loved the ragged gasp that ripped from his mouth. Soon, she added a second hand and double-fisted his length until Easy was using one of her shoulders for balance.

Scooting closer yet, Jenna leaned in and placed a long, flat lick up his whole length.

"Fuck, Jenna," he rasped, his hand stroking and petting her hair.

She licked him again and again and swirled her tongue around his head. The liquid gathered there was salty-sweet and filled her lower belly with a quivering pressure. Finally, she took his head between her lips, going slow to ease the sting of her cut and getting a feel for the size of him. He was heavy on her tongue, and she loved the sensation. Grasping his thigh for balance, Jenna slowly worked into a pattern using both her hand and her mouth to pleasure him. She looked up as much as she could, wanting to see his expression while she did this to him, but the dimness made it hard to see his eyes.

But all the clenching flinches of his ripped stomach muscles, all the bitten-out curses and groans, and the way his hands dove into her hair, played with her nipples, and caressed her face while he filled her cheeks spoke of a deeply pleasured man.

He grasped her jaw. "Oh, babe, you gotta stop."

She sucked up his length and gently let him drop from her mouth.

"Scoot back onto the bed," Easy said as he fished his wallet from his jeans and pulled something out. A condom wrapper, which he placed on the bed next to her.

He covered her with his big body, making her feel claimed, feminine, and totally enveloped by him. Kisses and caresses rained down over her face, her neck, her breasts. Jenna's heart thundered, and she trembled with the force of the desire flooding through her. It was unlike anything she'd ever experienced before, and she knew exactly why. She had an intense connection with Easy that made this so much more than two bodies or two friends coming together.

She hadn't known him long enough to be in love with him, but the affection she felt for him was so big, so deep, so intense, it filled her entire chest with a warm, elated pressure.

Easy dragged a hand down her stomach and gently played with the curls at the top of her sex. "You doing okay?" he asked.

"Yeah," she said, loving the way he checked in with her. She knew why he did it, and though she really felt mostly fine—especially with him—the extra care he took made her feel unquestionably confident about what she wanted to happen.

His mouth came down on hers as his fingers slid over the slick skin of her center.

Jenna cried out into the kiss as he spread her arousal

and stroked circles over the nerves at the top of her slit. She lifted her hips, seeking out more of him, *all* of him.

"Aw, you feel fucking fine," he said against her ear. And then he pushed his fingers down and slipped his middle finger inside.

"Oh, God," she said, the room spinning around her at the combination of his thick finger inside her and the heel of his hand grinding against her clit.

He added a second finger. "Babe, you are so fucking tight," Easy rasped.

She needed to tell him. Not because it would change anything about her decision but because it didn't feel fair to surprise a guy with her first-time reaction without having warned him first. "Easy?" she whispered.

"Yeah?" Pulling back to meet her gaze, he licked his lips. Desire hooded his dark eyes. And seeing it so plainly reflected there added another layer to her own arousal.

"I'm . . . this is . . . you are my first," she said, the admission making her stomach flip.

His eyebrows flew up, and he pulled his fingers out to brace himself above her. "Jesus, Jenna, are you sure you want it to be with me? Now? You only get to have this once. You don't have to do this. There's so much else we can do, we wouldn't have to stop."

Jenna placed her fingers on his lips. "I choose you, and I don't have a single doubt." She really didn't. For so many reasons, no guy would be more appropriate to share this with than him.

Brow furrowing, he shook his head. "I don't want to hurt you when you've already been hurt," he said, his voice full of grit.

"But after that, it'll feel so good," she whispered, hope and need flowing through her. "Right?"

Easy groaned, and his cock jerked against her hip. For a moment, a battle played out on his expression, and then he leaned down and kissed her, covering her with his body again. She loved the feeling of his weight on her and all around her. It was comforting and arousing at the same time. The kisses were sweet and hot, tender and urgent, and filled with a gratitude that made her heart swell in her chest.

When he broke away, he cupped her face and looked deep into her eyes. "You are very special to me, Jenna. I want you to know that."

She smiled, and her heart swelled impossibly more. "I feel it, Easy. And so are you, to me. Oh!" she said, smiling even bigger. "I keep forgetting to ask you, so I'm doing it now."

"Yeah?" he asked, the corners of his mouth lifting into a small, skeptical smile.

"What does 'Easy' stand for?"

He threw his head back and chuckled. "You want to know this now?"

She threaded her arms around his neck. "Well, yeah. Seems appropriate, don't you think?"

More laughter, and he kissed her on the nose, then the lips. "I guess so. My full name is Edward, Edward

Cantrell. 'Easy' came from my initials. Only one who calls me 'Edward' now is my father."

"Edward, huh?" she asked, trying his real name out for herself. Seemed really formal for the guy she'd come to know.

He shook his head and cocked an eyebrow. "Nuh-uh. Easy. After all these years, the nickname feels like the real me."

She grinned and nodded. "Yeah, I totally see that."

He kissed the side of her neck. "Anything else you'd like to know, Miss Dean?"

"No," she said, cupping and stroking the back of his neck and shoulders. Every part of him radiated power and strength. She could feel it above her, in her fingertips, in the way his muscles bunched and clenched.

"Good," he said, kissing her again and stroking his fingers down her body until they returned to her center. "I want to make sure you're ready for me."

The promise in those words had her pressing her hips into his touch.

"I want you to come for me, Jenna. I want to make this good for you."

Stroking her hands up over his short hair, she pulled his gaze to hers. "It's already perfect."

His fingers slipped inside her again, thrusting and stretching. "You're gonna feel so fucking good." He brought his wet fingertips to her clit again and swirled in fast circles.

Jenna gasped, thrust her hips, and held on to his shoulders, needing an anchor as her body spiraled tighter and tighter. "Oh my God, Easy," she said the intense, sweet pressure of a building orgasm stealing her breath and her mind.

"That's right, Jenna," he rasped.

Suddenly, she was right there, hanging off the edge of the cliff but not falling. "Oh, Oh, God." She whined and held her breath, pressing her hips harder against his hand.

Easy read her cues, apparently, because he rubbed harder.

Jenna came. A moan ripped out of her chest as she clutched Easy's shoulders and rode out wave after wave of pulsing sensation. When she returned to herself, she found Easy looking at her, and the adoration on his expression made her need him right that second.

As if hearing her thoughts, Easy gently pulled his hand away, reached for the condom, and pushed back onto his knees between her thighs. He placed the condom at his thick tip and rolled it down. Watching him do it was thrilling and arousing. Eyes locked on hers, he ran his fingers through her center and spread her wetness around the head.

"I'll take it slow, baby. Okay?"

"Yeah," she said, her heart rate tripping into a sprint anew.

And then he was right there, gently rubbing his tip through her wet folds and just penetrating her entrance before pulling away again. Finally, he pushed in just a little, and a little more. Jenna gasped and threw her head back. The sensation of stretching and fullness was intense and overwhelming, but not truly painful.

"Oh, fuck, fuck, fuck," Easy said in a rumble so low it was almost a growl. "I know you're small, but you were so made for me. Goddamnit. You okay?"

She blew out a breath. "Yes, you're just really big," she said, trying to breathe, trying to will herself open, trying to relax.

"I got you, I promise. I'll take it as slow as you need." And he did, so much so that his restraint set off a trembling in his muscles that was really freaking sexy because it meant he was desperate to have her. He pushed in farther, and Jenna moaned through the invasion.

The groan that spilled from his mouth when he bottomed out inside her made her wetter and more able to take him. As her body adjusted, the stillness of his body became almost too maddening to bear. "You can move," she whispered. "I'm okay."

Easy took her upper body in his arms and curled himself around her, and then his hips withdrew just a little. And with his movement, all that intense, overwhelming fullness transformed into something edgy and hot that felt good, then really good, then absolutely amazing.

Soon, his full strokes filled and retreated and her hips moved in time with his rhythm. "Aw, there it is babe. Fucking perfect," he said, his voice raw with desire. He kept his pace slow and tender, but the way he rolled his hips and leveraged against her shoulders made it so damn intense.

She'd *never* felt closer to another person in the world than she did to Easy right this moment. Emotion built up in her chest and tightened her throat, and Jenna surrendered herself to his kisses and his touch and the friction provided by his slowly swinging hips.

Of course, she didn't know how it was with other people, but making love with Easy was all-consuming. His warm spice in her nose, his incredibly sexy groans and rasps in her ears, and his hard muscles under her fingers and all around her. Just at that moment, nothing existed in the whole world except this place, this moment, this embrace.

"So amazing," she gasped against his cheek. "Want you so much."

"Aw, you have me. Have me, Jenna. Take me," he said, his thrusts getting faster but not harder.

Moans spilled out of her nonstop now, and even though the sensations she recognized as an orgasm weren't gathering in her belly, he felt so fucking good moving inside her, she wasn't concentrating on anything else.

His grip tightened as his hips moved faster, and a thrill shot through Jenna that she was able to hold this big man in her arms and give him so much pleasure, he literally fell apart. She yearned for his orgasm, wanting to feel it, to see it on his face.

A long, low groan, and he pressed a kiss to her uninjured cheek right in front of her ear. "I'm gonna come, Jenna. Because of you. Make me feel so fucking good."

She moaned, adoring the desire and need straining his words. "I wanna feel it," she said.

"Oh, baby, right now," he said. His hips crashed into hers once, twice, three times more, and he cried out. "Oh, fuck, Jenna." He slowed but didn't stop his movements, like he was teasing out his orgasm as long as he could. And Jenna was just fine with that because she wasn't in any hurry to lose him from inside her.

She threw her arms and legs around him and held on to him as hard as she could. "So glad it was you," she rasped, her throat suddenly tight.

He met her gaze when she finally released him. "Me, too, Jenna," he said, leaning in for a series of sweet, reverent kisses. "Be right back," he said, withdrawing from her.

Jenna hated to lose his weight and warmth and touch, but everything in her gut told her what'd just happened was their happy beginning.

And there was absolutely nothing she could regret about that.

Chapter 10

EASY LOOKED AT himself in the bathroom mirror as he washed his hands. *You will beat this fucking thing. For you. For her. For everything you could be together.*

Because he'd never experienced anything as intense and emotional as what he'd just shared with Jenna.

Part of it was that she'd been a virgin, and he'd felt the honor of that gift in his very soul. Part of it was the conversation they'd had just before, and the fact that he'd come to her in fear and despair and found only acceptance. And part of it was that he had feelings for this girl unlike anything he'd felt in a long, long time. Maybe ever.

Would he say it was love?

Maybe. Or maybe it made him feel so much better than he had in ages that it just felt like it could be that deep.

But he'd definitely be willing to say it was heading in that direction.

He dried his hands and darted back down the hall.

He didn't want to rush anything with Jenna, though, because she was right. Neither of them were in the best headspace right now. Both of them needed time to heal and regroup from the shit hands they'd been dealt. But they could make those journeys side by side. And whatever grew along the way? Easy would be ready for and open to it.

Back in bed, he loved that Jenna rolled right in against him, filling the space alongside his body like it was made for her and her alone.

He stroked the hair back from her face, careful to avoid the bruises, and looked into her blue eyes. "You okay, babe?"

Her eyes went glassy on a quick nod. "Yeah. More than," she said.

Easy caught a tear with his thumb, a rock taking up form in his gut. "What are these for, then?"

Her breath caught and shuddered, and her struggle to fight against whatever this was threatened to break his heart. "It's just that . . . I could've missed this, with you. If you hadn't gotten me—"

"Aw, no. I got you then. I have you now." He squeezed her in tight.

"I know. I know you do," she said, sniffling. "I really care about you, Easy. I can't imagine never having found you. I just want you to know that you are so important to me."

"I feel the same way. I'm gonna get myself well and you're gonna heal and my guys are gonna figure out all this other bullshit, and then it'll be you and me."

"Best plan ever," she said, snuggling in against his neck.

Easy chuckled. "I'll fucking second that."

EASY WOKE UP as if slowly surfacing from underwater. He'd been down so deep, he was foggy-headed and heavy-limbed, and a quick bleary-eyed scan of him and Jenna said neither of them had moved an inch since they'd fallen asleep. However long ago that was.

His internal alarm clock said it'd been a long time, and it was late now, but he couldn't remember exactly where his phone had landed, and he wasn't about to wake Jenna to look.

That thought led him to another—the soul-deep comfort of waking with another person in his arms. So much of what had hurt the past twelve months was the total isolation, the constant aloneness with his thoughts, the feeling that no one would notice if he were gone. But between Jenna and the guys and the new friends he'd made here, it was like they'd each reached into his chest, picked up a broken shard of his heart, and put it back into place.

It was a first step.

Jenna stretched against him, all that soft skin dragging along his. His dick took immediate notice and wanted to say good morning, but he didn't want her to think that sex was what he thought they were all about. Plus, she was probably sore.

"Hi," she whispered, as her hand landed on his chest.

Her fingers drew patterns over his skin that were as sweet as they were arousing.

"Hi, sleepyhead."

"Yeah," she said, a smile in her voice. She stretched again, her hips rubbing against his. Easy had to bite back a groan. "How are you?" she asked in that same half-awake tone.

"Feeling pretty good." And it was true. He was even smiling.

"Me, too." She yawned. "I was thinking maybe I should rejoin the world today. Meet everybody and stuff."

"We can definitely make that happen," he said. "But let me ask how you want to deal with us around everyone else. No pressure at all. It'll be hard as hell to keep my hands off you all day, but I'll gladly do it for you." He pressed a kiss to her forehead.

She smiled. "I don't mind people knowing, Easy. Besides, these people are all your friends, right?"

"My best friends," he said. "My chosen family." He knew that was true down deep. "And you're part of that too, now."

Jenna kissed to his chest. "You're a sweet, sweet man, Easy. Don't worry, though. I won't tell."

He chuckled. "Good. Let's just keep that between you and me." As they lay in each other's arms, an idea came to mind, one that had been rolling around in his head since he'd arrived here, but Easy hadn't known what exactly to do before. Now he knew. "After we meet everyone and eat, will you do something with me?"

"Anything," Jenna said without a moment's hesitation.

Her agreement made him eager to get a move on.

They took a shower filled with slow kisses and hot caresses, and apparently showering with a man was a first for her, too. He couldn't deny the masculine satisfaction he felt from being her first, but a part of him said it would be even more significant to be her last.

Afterward, Jenna picked out another of his shirts. Really, that would never get old. Downstairs, Easy made the rounds, reintroducing the guys she'd met under pressure at Confessions days before, and introducing others who hadn't been there for the first time.

Jenna ate enough for breakfast to get back on her medicine, and that was a load off everyone's mind. Shane informed Easy that he'd solved the antidepressants problem by calling his longtime family doc from back home, explaining that he was on business travel, and pretending that Easy's symptoms were his own. The prescription would be ready to pick up later today. It sucked that was the way they had to do it, but lying was the lesser of two evils in this particular situation. And it just proved again what good friends he had.

Finally, hand in hand, Easy took Jenna down the steps to Hard Ink and found Jeremy at a table sketching. "Got a second?" Easy asked.

"Yeah, man, always," he said, closing his book.

Jenna started laughing, and Easy tracked her gaze to where it settled on Jer's shirt, which read in all caps, "I LIKE TO SNATCH KISSES. AND VICE VERSA."

Easy snickered. "Better get used to it. He has an unending supply of them."

"Good to know," Jenna said, grinning.

Jeremy winked at her. "So whatcha need?"

"Some ink."

The guy rubbed his hands together, and his face lit up like it was Christmas. "Finally, I get my hands on one of you." And then he did an approximation of an evil laugh.

Waggling his eyebrows, Jeremy said, "I can totally do you now, or at least get you started. How big?"

"Not very," Easy said. "It's words."

"Wait here, then." He returned a moment later with a few sheets of laminated paper. "Tell me if there's a font here you want to work from or if you want me to make something totally else up."

Within fifteen minutes, he was in a chair in Jeremy's tattoo room, shirt off, skin prepared, and Jenna by his side. Easy felt good. He needed the reminder. He needed the affirmation. And he wanted to make a commitment so strong it was written in his very skin.

"Ready?" Jeremy asked.

"Can't believe I'm letting a Rixey take a gun to me," Easy muttered. "But, yeah, I guess so."

"Ha," Jeremy said, smiling. "You're in good hands here."

"Then let's do it."

Jenna kept a hand on Easy's knee while she watched Jeremy go to work. "Does it hurt?" she asked.

"Not really," he said, even though, truth be told, the needles did bite into his rib cage. But it was a small price to pay. And a helluva lot less painful than what he'd been carrying around.

The three of them chatted while Jeremy worked, *especially* Jeremy. And that was okay because he made Jenna laugh until she cried so many times that the skin around her eyes was red. And it was also good because it distracted her from a little something extra he'd asked Jeremy to do.

About an hour later, it was all done. "Take a look," Jeremy said.

"Oh, it's gorgeous," Jenna said, voice full of pride and awe.

Easy held up the mirror and got a good look at the words along the right side of his rib cage in dark, crisp black. Words he remembered from a large plaque hanging in his church back home. He didn't attend much anymore, but the words had always stuck with him. Now it was almost like they were *for* him.

YOU WERE NEVER
CREATED TO LIVE
DEPRESSED,
DEFEATED, GUILTY,
CONDEMNED, ASHAMED
OR UNWORTHY.
YOU WERE CREATED
TO BE
VICTORIOUS.

The knot in Easy's throat only got tighter when he read the line of initials in much smaller lettering that ran beneath:

M.R. E.Z. J.H. W.A. C.E. C.K.

The initials of his six fallen teammates. Below that line, a piece of gauze was taped to his side, hiding something special he'd thrown in, something he didn't want Jenna to see just yet.

The first tattoo was for himself. The second so that his friends would know he'd never forgotten, and never could.

"It's fucking perfect, Jeremy," he said, unable to keep how moved he was out of his voice at actually seeing those words and those initials a permanent part of his skin.

Jeremy clapped him on the back. "So glad to hear it, man. Happy to do more anytime."

After Easy got all his instructions and settled up, he pulled Jenna into the hallway outside Hard Ink, shirt in hand.

"What you did is beautiful, Easy. I'm really proud of you," Jenna said, looking up at him with more of that adoration that made him feel like he could do anything. Beat anything.

"There's something else, too," he said, turning his bare side to her. Now that they were alone, he needed her to see. "Take off the gauze."

"What?" she asked, her gaze flashing between his face and his ink. "I'll hurt you."

"You won't. Please?"

"Okay," she said, and she slowly peeled the tape from his skin.

Easy's chest filled with a restless anticipation of her reaction.

She gasped. "Oh, Easy."

He knew what she'd find there. A third tattoo, this time in red ink. It had just two words:

I believe.

From what she'd said last night, and made him say, too. *I believe that Jenna believes in the good in me and always will.* Easy wanted Jenna to know, no matter what became of them, she would never stop being important to him for the belief she'd given him with her words, her heart, and her body.

Together, the three pieces seemed to snap another piece of the puzzle of his heart back into place. Just like building a wall. Brick by brick.

He could work with that.

"What do you think?" he finally asked as he turned to her.

She tackle hugged him so hard that he stumbled back a step before he caught her in his arms and lifted her until she wrapped her legs around his hips.

"It's the most amazing thing I've ever seen. I can't believe you put my words on your body with that beautiful saying and your friends' names." She gave him the sweetest kiss and leaned her forehead against his. "But why is it in red?"

He met her questioning gaze with a smile. "For you, and all this beautiful red hair."

"Oh," she said, voice tight. "Oh, my God. How do you expect me not to tell people how sweet you are when you do this?"

He chuckled, then he got serious again. "I believe, Jenna," he said, referring to her affirming words, but feeling a whole lot more. For her. "Or, at least, I'll keep saying it until it's true."

"Oh, Easy," she whispered against his lips. "I'll be right there with you, because I believe, too."

Author's Note

WRITING ABOUT A suicidal character is one of the most challenging things I've ever done, but also one of the most important. Suicide is always tragic, but it has become an epidemic among American active-duty service members and veterans alike. The statistics are staggering and heart-wrenching. In the U.S. Army, which has the highest suicide rate among the branches (48.7 percent of all military suicides in 2012), the suicide rate in 2012 was thirty per hundred thousand, compared with fourteen per hundred thousand among civilians and eighteen per hundred thousand in 2008. In 2012, 841 active-duty service members attempted or committed suicide. Among veterans, as of November 2013, twenty-two committed suicide every day. Every. Day. A frightening 30 percent of veterans say they've considered suicide, and 45 percent say they know an Iraq or Afghanistan veteran who has attempted or committed suicide.

In a study of veterans, combat-related guilt was the most significant predictor of suicide attempts and of preoccupation with suicide after discharge. Veterans' suicidal thoughts are also related to feelings that one does not belong with other people or has become a burden. Couple these sad realities with the fact that veterans are less likely to seek care than active-duty military or civilians, and you begin to understand why statistics like these exist.

Suicide is a process that begins with ideas and thoughts, followed by planning, and finally followed by a suicidal act. If you or someone you love is experiencing these thoughts, please seek immediate medical help or call the Suicide Prevention Hotline at 1-800-273-8255 (TALK). This service works with civilians of all ages, active-duty military, and veterans.

I hope Easy's story raises awareness of the problems these brave men and women—and our country as a whole—face. But awareness is not enough. Therefore, I will be donating all of my proceeds from the first two weeks' sales of this book (8/19/14 – 9/1/14) to a national non-profit that assists wounded veterans. Because I don't want anyone else's Edward "Easy" Cantrell to be one of the twenty-two, either.

Acknowledgments

I'M SO HAPPY that Easy got his story and that my awesome editor Amanda Bergeron agreed it needed to be told! Many thanks to her and the whole team at Avon for her incredible support of the Hard Ink series. Many thanks also to my agent Kevan Lyon for being such an amazing source of support and guidance, and to my publicist KP Simmon at InkSlinger PR for loving these guys, supporting me, and cheering me on.

I must absolutely thank my good friend Christi Barth, an awesome author in her own right, for reading the manuscript and offering such useful comments and feedback. Christi has read every word in the Hard Ink world, and these stories wouldn't be what they are without her. Thank you, Christi!

I also want to thank Dr. Jeffrey Goodie for providing me with reports and information about suicide in the military. Jeff is a clinical health psychologist in the U.S.

Public Health Service who served in the U.S. Air Force for nine years. (He was also my husband's college roommate and our family's good friend!)

Next, I want to thank my husband Brian and our daughters for all their amazing support. I couldn't write a word without it, and I appreciate it from the bottom of my heart.

Finally, I want to thank you, the readers, for welcoming characters into your hearts and minds and letting them tell their stories over and over again. It's all for you. And you're the best!

~LK

The Hard Ink series continues . . .
HARD TO COME BY
A Hard Ink Novel

Caught between desire and loyalty . . .

Derek DiMarzio would do anything for the members of his disgraced Special Forces team—sacrifice his body, help a former teammate with a covert operation to restore their honor, and even go behind enemy lines. He just never expected to want the beautiful woman he found there.

When a sexy stranger asks questions about her brother, Emilie Garza is torn between loyalty to the brother she once idolized and fear of the war-changed man he's become. Derek's easy smile and quiet strength tempt Emilie to open up, igniting the desire between them and leading Derek to crave a woman he shouldn't trust.

As the team's investigation reveals how powerful their enemies are, Derek and Emilie must prove where their loyalties lie before hearts are broken and lives are lost. Because love is too hard to come by to let slip away . . .

Available everywhere December 2014

About the Author

LAURA KAYE IS the *New York Times* and *USA Today* bestselling author of over a dozen books in contemporary and paranormal romance and romantic suspense. Laura grew up amid family lore involving angels, ghosts, and evil-eye curses, cementing her life-long fascination with storytelling and the supernatural. Laura lives in Maryland with her husband, two daughters, and cute-but-bad dog, and appreciates her view of the Chesapeake Bay every day.

Visit www.AuthorTracker.com for exclusive information on your favorite HarperCollins authors.

Give in to your impulses . . .
Read on for a sneak peek at three brand-new
e-book original tales of romance
from Avon Books.
Available now wherever e-books are sold.

FULL EXPOSURE
BOOK ONE: INDEPENDENCE FALLS
By Sara Jane Stone

PERSONAL TARGET
AN ELITE OPS NOVEL
By Kay Thomas

SINFUL REWARDS 1
A BILLIONAIRES AND BIKERS NOVELLA
By Cynthia Sax

An Excerpt from

FULL EXPOSURE
Book One: Independence Falls
by Sara Jane Stone

The first book in a hot new series from
contemporary romance writer Sara Jane
Stone. When Georgia begins work as a
nanny for her brother's best friend, she
knows she can't have him, but his pull is
too strong, and she feels sparks igniting.

GEORGIA TRULANE WALKED into the kitchen wearing a purple bikini, hoping and praying for a reaction from the man she'd known practically forever. Seated at the kitchen table, Eric Moore, her brother's best friend, now her boss since she'd taken over the care of his adopted nephew until he found another live-in nanny, studied his laptop as if it held the keys to the world's greatest mysteries. Unless the answers were listed between items b and c on a spreadsheet about Oregon timber harvesting, the screen was not of earth-shattering importance. It certainly did not merit his full attention when she was wearing an itsy-bitsy string bikini.

"Nate is asleep," she said.

Look up. Please, look up.

Eric nodded, his gaze fixed to the screen. Why couldn't he look at her with that unwavering intensity? He'd snuck glances. There had been moments when she'd turned from preparing his nephew's lunch and caught him looking at her, really looking, as if he wanted to memorize the curve of her neck or the way her jeans fit. But he quickly turned away.

"Did you pick up everything he needs for his first day of school tomorrow? I don't want to send him unprepared."

His deep voice warmed her from the inside out. It was so familiar and welcoming, yet at the same time utterly sexy.

"I got all the items on the list," she said. "He is packed and ready to go."

"He needs another one of those stuffed frogs. He can't go without his favorite stuffed animal."

If she hadn't been standing in his kitchen practically naked, waiting for him to notice her, she would have found his concern for the three-year-old's first day of pre-school sweet, maybe even heartwarming. But her body wasn't looking for sentiments reminiscent of sunshine and puppies, or the whisper of sweet nothings against her skin. She craved physical contact—his hands on her, exploring, each touch making her feel more alive.

And damn it, he still hadn't glanced up from his laptop.

"Nate will be home by nap time," she said. "He'll be there for only a few hours. You know that, right?"

"He'll want to take his frog," he said, his fingers moving across the keyboard. "He'll probably lose it. And he sleeps with that thing every night. He needs that frog."

She might be practically naked, but his emphasis on the word *need* thrust her headfirst into heartwarming territory. Eric worked day and night to provide Nate with the stability that had been missing from Eric's childhood thanks to his divorced parents' fickle dating habits. She admired his willingness to put a child who'd suffered a tragic loss first.

But tonight, for one night, she didn't want to think

about all of his honorable qualities. She wanted to see if maybe, just maybe those stolen glances when he thought she wasn't looking meant that the man she'd laid awake thinking about while serving her country half a world away wanted her too.

"You're now the proud owner of two stuffed frogs," she said. "So if that's everything for tonight, I'm going for a swim."

Finally, *finally*, he looked up. She watched as his blue eyes widened and his jaw clenched. He was an imposing man, large and strong from years of climbing and felling trees. Not that he did the grunt work anymore. These days he wore tailored suits and spent more time in an office than with a chainsaw in hand. But even seated at his kitchen table poring over a computer, he looked like a wall of strong, solid muscle wound tight and ready for action. Having all of that energy focused on her? It sent a thrill down her body. Georgia clung to the feeling, savoring it.

An Excerpt from

PERSONAL TARGET
An Elite Ops Novel
by Kay Thomas

One minute Jennifer Grayson is housesitting
and the next she's abducted to a foreign brothel.
Jennifer is planning her escape when her first
"customer" arrives. Nick, the man who broke
her heart years ago, has come to her rescue.
Now, as they race for their lives, passion for
each other reignites and old secrets resurface.
Can Nick keep the woman he loves safe
against an enemy with a personal vendetta?

THE WOMAN AT the vanity turned, and his breath caught in his throat. Nick had known it would be Jenny, and despite what he'd thought about downstairs when he'd seen her on the tablet screen, he hadn't prepared himself for seeing her like this. Seated at the table with candles all around, she was wearing a sheer robe over a grey thong and a bustier kind of thing—or that's what he thought the full-length bra was called.

He spotted the unicorn tat peeping out from the edge of whatever the lingerie piece was, and his brain quit processing details as all the blood in his head rushed south. He'd been primed to come in and tell Jenny exactly how they were getting out of the house and away from these people, and now . . . this. His mouth went dry at the sight of her. She looked like every fantasy he'd ever had about her rolled into one.

He continued to stare as recognition flared in her eyes.

"Oh my god," she murmured. "It's . . ."

She clapped her mouth closed, and her eyes widened. That struck him as odd. The relief on her face was obvious, but instead of looking at him, she took an audible breath and studied the walls of the room. When she finally did glance at him again, her eyes had changed.

"So you're who they've sent me for my first time?" Her voice sounded bored, not the tone he remembered. "What do you want me to do?"

What a question. He raised an eyebrow, but she shook her head. In warning?

Nothing here was as he'd anticipated. He continued staring at her, hoping the lust would quit fogging his brain long enough for him to figure out what was going on.

"I've been told to show you a good time." Her voice was cold, downright chilly. Without another word she stood and crossed the floor, slipping into his arms with her breasts pressing into his chest. "It's you." She murmured the words in the barest of whispers.

Nick's mind froze, but his body didn't. His hands automatically went to her waist as she kissed his neck, working her way up to his ear. This was not at all what he'd planned.

"I can't believe you're here." She breathed the words into his ear.

Me either, he thought, but kept the words to himself as he pulled her closer. His senses flooded with all that smooth skin pressing against him. His body tightened, and his right hand moved to cup her ass. Her cheek's bare skin was silky soft, just like he remembered. God, he'd missed her. She melted into him as his body switched into overdrive.

"What do you want?" She spoke louder. The arctic tone was back. He was confused and knew he was just too stupid with wanting her to figure out what the hell was going on. There was no way the woman could mistake the effect she was having.

She moved her lips closer to his ear and nipped his earlobe as she whispered, "Cameras are everywhere. I'm not sure about microphones."

And like that, cold reality slapped him in the face. He should have been expecting it, but he'd been so focused on getting her out and making sure she was all right. She might be glad to see him because he was there to save her, but throwing her body at him was an act.

Jesus. He had to get them both out of here without tipping his hand to the cameras and those watching what he was doing. He was crazy not to have considered it once he saw those tablets downstairs, but it had never occurred to him that he would have to play this encounter through as if he were really a client.

He slipped her arms from around his neck and moved to the table to pour himself some wine, willing his hands not to shake. "I want you," he said.

An Excerpt from

SINFUL REWARDS 1
A Billionaires and Bikers Novella
by Cynthia Sax

Belinda "Bee" Carter is a good girl; at least,
that's what she tells herself. And a good girl
deserves a nice guy—just like the gorgeous
and moody billionaire Nicolas Rainer. Or
so she thinks, until she takes a look through
her telescope and sees a naked, tattooed man
on the balcony across the courtyard. He has
been watching her, and that makes him all
the more enticing. But when a mysterious
and anonymous text message dares her to
do something bad, she must decide if she is
really the good girl she has always claimed
to be, or if she's willing to risk everything
for her secret fantasy of being watched.

An Avon Red Novella

I'D TOLD CYNDI I'd never use it, that it was an instrument purchased by perverts to spy on their neighbors. She'd laughed and called me a prude, not knowing that I was one of those perverts, that I secretly yearned to watch and be watched, to care and be cared for.

If I'm cautious, and I'm always cautious, she'll never realize I used her telescope this morning. I swing the tube toward the bench and adjust the knob, bringing the mysterious object into focus.

It's a phone. Nicolas's phone. I bounce on the balls of my feet. This is a sign, another declaration from fate that we belong together. I'll return Nicolas's much-needed device to him. As a thank you, he'll invite me to dinner. We'll talk. He'll realize how perfect I am for him, fall in love with me, marry me.

Cyndi will find a fiancé also—everyone loves her—and we'll have a double wedding, as sisters of the heart often do. It'll be the first wedding my family has had in generations.

Everyone will watch us as we walk down the aisle. I'll wear a strapless white Vera Wang mermaid gown with organza and lace details, crystal and pearl embroidery accents, the bodice fitted, and the skirt hemmed for my shorter height. My hair will be swept up. My shoes—

Voices murmur outside the condo's door, the sound piercing my delightful daydream. I swing the telescope upward, not wanting to be caught using it. The snippets of conversation drift away.

I don't relax. If the telescope isn't positioned in the same way as it was last night, Cyndi will realize I've been using it. She'll tease me about being a fellow pervert, sharing the story, embellished for dramatic effect, with her stern, serious dad—or, worse, with Angel, that snobby friend of hers.

I'll die. It'll be worse than being the butt of jokes in high school because that ridicule was about my clothes and this will center on the part of my soul I've always kept hidden. It'll also be the truth, and I won't be able to deny it. I am a pervert.

I have to return the telescope to its original position. This is the only acceptable solution. I tap the metal tube.

Last night, my man-crazy roommate was giggling over the new guy in three-eleven north. The previous occupant was a gray-haired, bowtie-wearing tax auditor, his luxurious accommodations supplied by Nicolas. The most exciting thing he ever did was drink his tea on the balcony.

According to Cyndi, the new occupant is a delicious piece of man candy—tattooed, buff, and head-to-toe lickable. He was completing armcurls outside, and she enthusiastically counted his reps, oohing and aahing over his bulging biceps, calling to me to take a look.

I resisted that temptation, focusing on making macaroni and cheese for the two of us, the recipe snagged from the diner my mom works in. After we scarfed down dinner, Cyndi licking her plate clean, she left for the club and hasn't returned.

Three-eleven north is the mirror condo to ours. I straighten the telescope. That position looks about right, but then, the imitation UGGS I bought in my second year of college looked about right also. The first time I wore the boots in the rain, the sheepskin fell apart, leaving me barefoot in Economics 201.

Unwilling to risk Cyndi's friendship on "about right," I gaze through the eyepiece. The view consists of rippling golden planes, almost like . . .

Tanned skin pulled over defined abs.

I blink. It can't be. I take another look. A perfect pearl of perspiration clings to a puckered scar. The drop elongates more and more, stretching, snapping. It trickles downward, navigating the swells and valleys of a man's honed torso.

No. I straighten. This is wrong. I shouldn't watch our sexy neighbor as he stands on his balcony. If anyone catches me . . .